M000119352

Warrior

Anna Hackett

Warrior

Published by Anna Hackett
Copyright 2016 by Anna Hackett
Cover by Melody Simmons of eBookindiecovers
Edits by Tanya Saari

ISBN (eBook): 978-1-925539-06-6
ISBN (paperback): 978-1-925539-11-0

What readers are saying about Anna's Science Fiction Romance

Galactic Gladiators – Most Original Story Universe Winner 2016 – Gravetells

Gladiator – Two-time winner for Best Sci-fi Romance 2016 – Gravetells and Under the Covers

Hell Squad – Amazon Bestselling Science Fiction Romance Series and SFR Galaxy Award for best Post-Apocalypse for Readers who don't like Post-Apocalypse

At Star's End – One of Library Journal's Best E-Original Romances for 2014

Return to Dark Earth – One of Library Journal's Best E-Original Books for 2015 and two-time SFR Galaxy Awards winner

The Phoenix Adventures – SFR Galaxy Award Winner for Most Fun New Series and "Why Isn't This a Movie?" Series

Beneath a Trojan Moon – RWAus Ella Award Winner for Romantic Novella of the Year

"Like Indiana Jones meets Star Wars. A treasure hunt with a steamy romance." – SFF Dragon, review of *Among Galactic Ruins*

"Strap in, enjoy the heat of romance and the daring of this group of space travellers!" – Di, Top 500 Amazon Reviewer, review of *At Star's End*

"High action and adventure surrounding an impossible treasure hunt kept me reading until late in the night." – Jen, That's What I'm Talking About, review of *Beyond Galaxy's Edge*

"Action, danger, aliens, romance – yup, it's another great book from Anna Hackett!" – Book Gannet Reviews, review of *Hell Squad: Marcus*

Don't miss out! For updates about new releases, action romance info, free books, and other fun stuff, sign up for my VIP mailing list and get your *free box set* containing three action-packed romances.

Visit here to get started:
www.annahackettbooks.com

Chapter One

The roar of the crowd was electrifying.

Regan Forrest felt the hairs on her arms rise. She could feel the excitement and energy pumping off the crowd sitting in the stands around her. Some people were chanting, others were shouting out the names of their favorite gladiators, waiting for the fight to begin.

As she scanned the huge, old stone arena, she could almost imagine she was sitting back in the Colosseum in Ancient Rome. But then she blinked, and saw the different alien species sitting on the tiered seats. She heard the roar of engines, as a giant starship shot overhead, taking off from the nearby spaceport.

No, she was nowhere near Earth.

Instead, she'd been abducted by alien slavers and transported to the other side of the galaxy.

The warm cream stone of the Kor Magna Arena might be old and worn through hundreds of years of gladiatorial fights, but around her, people were holding high-tech devices: communicators, binoculars, and who knew what else. Most of the technology wouldn't have looked out of place on the space station where she worked.

Correction. Where she *had* worked. She swallowed, her throat tightening. The Fortuna Space Station orbiting Jupiter probably didn't even exist anymore after the Thraxians had attacked it. Regan still couldn't believe that she'd gone from botanist to slave in the blink of an eye.

You're free now, Regan. She stared up. Free, but still light years from Earth, with no way to get home. She blinked as bright strobe lights hit her eyes. The arena's lights were coming on, even though the sun hadn't quite set. *Correction.* Suns. She watched the huge dual suns of Kor Magna sinking over the walls of the arena, heading toward the horizon of the desert planet.

Everything closed in on her. The noise thundered in her head, disorienting her. Her heart raced, and she shifted in her seat, trying to find some calm. The Thraxians had kept her locked up in a cell on their ship for so long, that now, sitting here surrounded by thousands of screaming people was too much. She felt a trickle of sweat roll down her spine, and once again, she looked up at the sky. But the two giant suns just reminded her that she wasn't on Earth and never would be again.

"Are you okay, Regan?"

The voice beside her instantly made the pressure in her head ease. She smiled at her friend Harper and reminded herself that no matter how bad things seemed, she wasn't alone. "Getting there." She nodded toward the stands. "This is pretty crazy, isn't it?"

Her friend smiled and bumped her shoulder

against Regan's. "It's insane. But you'll get used to it." Harper's eagle-eyed gaze moved back down to the sand-covered floor of the arena, anticipation on her face. "The fights can be brutal, but there is no doubt that they're also amazing."

Regan managed a nod. Harper was her best friend, and the space marine had also been snatched off the space station. But while Regan was still trying to put on the weight she'd lost in captivity and negotiate this strange new world, Harper looked...great.

With her tall, athletic body and sleek, dark hair, Harper was glowing. She wore dark-leather pants and a leather vest that showed off her toned arms, as well as the gorgeous alien tattoos on her left one.

A symbol that one of the big, tough gladiators who was about to step into the arena had claimed her.

Regan still couldn't quite believe her friend had fallen in love with an alien gladiator, but she couldn't dispute the fact that Harper had found a place here in Kor Magna. She'd found a home, a place in the arena, and love. She wasn't just surviving, she was thriving.

And perhaps Regan could, as well.

She shifted in her seat again. Maybe. Galen, the Imperator of the House of Galen, had taken her in when Harper and his gladiators had rescued her. The intimidating man was in charge of everything to do with his House. He'd given her a room to stay in, and recently, another small space where she'd set up a small lab. She'd been going crazy doing

3

nothing, and unlike Harper, who was trained in security and fighting, Regan couldn't even hold a sword, let alone fight in the arena.

Analyzing some of the fascinating alien substances she'd come across was keeping her sane. Her lab was her own little oasis in the midst of chaos.

For a brief second, she thought of her parents back on Earth. Did they miss her? Were they grieving for her? Pain seared her heart. No, probably not. Her parents had disowned her long before she'd been abducted.

The cries of the crowd rose to deafening levels. Around them, lots of people leaped to their feet, waving their hands in the air.

"Here they come," Harper said.

They were sitting in the seats assigned to the House of Galen, right up close to the arena floor. Regan had a perfect view as the gladiators entered.

She felt a lick of excitement. She knew exactly who she was waiting to see.

Saff strode in first. The female gladiator had it all—muscled body, glossy dark skin, and black hair pulled back in an abundance of braids. She raised an arm above her head, waving at the crowd. In her other hand, she was holding something small. Regan knew Saff's weapon of choice was a special kind of net, as well as the short sword attached to her belt.

The House of Galen's gladiators all worked in pairs, and Saff's partner followed her in. Kace was about as clean-cut as a gladiator got, with bronze skin and a detailed, leather arm guard over his right shoulder and muscled bicep. He had a handsome, hard-planed face. He nodded to the crowd, his long metal staff held in one strong hand.

Another pair of gladiators stepped out onto the sand. Regan didn't know these two as well, but both were tall. Lore was far leaner, with a long fall of tawny hair, while his partner, Nero, was a huge mountain of a gladiator. Lore turned in a circle and threw something in the air. A small cloud of smoke rose up, before fireworks shot up into the sky.

The crowd cheered and Nero scowled.

Lore was an illusionist, and used his tricks to charm the crowd. He'd told Regan that everything that happened in the arena was just one big show.

Then, the final pair of House of Galen gladiators stepped out of the tunnel and entered the arena. The roar of the crowd exploded.

Beside Regan, Harper let out a sharp whistle. Regan looked at Raiden first. Every tattooed, hard inch of him. He wore simple leather straps across his chest, which were attached to a blood-red cloak that fell down his back. Tattoos in black ink covered his arms and chest. He was an imposing sight, champion of the arena, and loved by all the spectators. He didn't even glance at the crowd. He was there to fight.

Then Regan saw *him*.

Raiden's partner was a huge warrior called Thorin.

Big, broad shoulders and a hard chest crisscrossed with dark leather. He was all corded

ANNA HACKETT

muscle, and his rugged face was set off by his shaved head. He smiled for the crowd, lifting a huge axe up in one hand.

He had big hands. Rough hands. She'd studied those hands closely when he'd carried her off the Thraxian slave ship. And she'd studied them a lot over the last few weeks, as she'd settled in at the House of Galen.

Thorin played to the crowd, turning in a slow circle. She took in the back view of him. Dark-brown leather trousers clung to him. The man had a magnificent ass and legs like tree trunks. He was just so masculine, rugged, and a little wild. He fascinated her.

Regan shifted in her seat. After two weeks in the House of Galen, she knew she was safe. She was no longer stuck in a cell, starving, or being beaten. She felt like she was waking up from a nightmare, slowly coming back to life.

Looking at Thorin made something else inside her come back to life, too.

He finished his circle and stopped. That was when she realized he was looking at her.

As their gazes connected, Regan felt a zip of electricity race through her. She lifted a hand in greeting.

He gave her one short nod before he turned to join the other gladiators.

Regan let out a shaky breath. She was a sensible scientist, and she'd been raised by strict parents who were always concerned with what the neighbors thought. Never in her entire life had

6

Regan felt the urge to climb a man's huge, muscled body and wrap her legs around his waist, but she did now. Boy, did she ever.

The voices of the announcers echoed through the arena, and thanks to the language translator device the Thraxians had implanted in her head, she had no trouble understanding their words.

The competitors had entered the arena.

As she saw the opposing gladiators come out of the tunnel on the opposite side of the arena, her muscles locked tight.

Tonight, the House of Galen were fighting their bitter rivals—the House of Thrax.

The same aliens who had abducted Regan and Harper, and however many others from Fortuna. Her hands twisted together. She knew her cousin Rory, an engineer on the space station, was here, somewhere. She'd been a prisoner of the Thraxians but had been moved before she could be rescued.

We'll find you, Rory. I promise. Harper had also seen the civilian commander of the space station, Madeline Cochran, get snatched too. But so far, despite the best efforts of the House of Galen gladiators, there had been no sign of the women.

Regan tried to pull a breath into her constricted lungs. Her gaze zeroed in on the gladiators below. Not all the gladiators for the House of Thrax were Thraxians, but a few were. She easily picked them out. They looked like the demons they were. Massive bodies covered in toughened, dark-brown skin, a set of sharp horns that protruded from the top of their heads, and small tusks on either side of their mouths. Even from this distance, she saw the faint glow of orange veins under their skin.

For a second, the arena swam, and Regan was back in her cell. Her stomach turned over, and she thought she might be sick. Then she blinked, and saw Thorin watching her again. As her gaze flicked to the Thraxian gladiators and then back to him, she saw his face harden.

The Thraxians worshipped strength and might above all else, and they saw nothing wrong with being cruel to those beneath them. As a small, puny woman from a backward planet like Earth, they'd seen her as no better than an ant. Completely worthless.

Harper leaned forward. "The fight's about to begin."

A siren sounded deafeningly—the long, mournful wail of a horn.

The House of Thrax gladiators charged forward, roaring battle cries. The House of Galen gladiators spread out a little, their feet shoulder width apart, holding their weapons easily, like natural extensions of their bodies.

Regan watched the gladiators clash together. Raiden, Thorin, and the others hit hard. There were no soft blows, just bone-rattling hit after hit, and soon, she saw gladiators stumbling, and blood splattering on the sand.

She pressed a hand to her tight stomach. She reminded herself that this wasn't a fight to the death. Here in Kor Magna, the gladiator houses spent a small fortune purchasing, training, and caring for their gladiators. They made a lot of money in the arena and from corporate sponsorship, so losing a gladiator was bad all around.

But that didn't mean there weren't a lot of injuries—bad ones. Harper had told her that the houses also spent a lot of money on medical technology to ensure the gladiators could be patched up after each fight.

She watched as Thorin swung his axe. They'd be fine. All of them. She knew they'd been fighting in the arena for a very long time.

Thorin took down one of the Thraxians. He charged past the throng of fighters, and then spotted a smaller, frightened gladiator. The young man had a long, narrow build and was holding an axe that looked far too heavy for him. He was shaking in terror.

Thorin gripped the man's arm and pushed him toward Raiden. Raiden said something and then pushed the man back behind the House of Galen gladiators. The smaller man fell into the sand, crying.

This was another reason Regan felt so safe at the House of Galen. These big, tough fighters also had the need to protect in their bones. Harper had told her they made it their mission to clandestinely help weaker fighters who ended up in the arena.

Thorin charged a larger, taller gladiator. His axe slammed against the sword of the big fighter, shattering it. She watched, mesmerized, as he plowed through his opponents.

That's when she realized he was targeting only the gladiators who were of the Thraxian species. Her breath hitched. He was taking down each gladiator who was of the species who'd stolen and abused her. She pressed a fist to her chest, feeling her heart knocking against her ribs.

No one had ever fought for her before.

A second Thraxian came in from the side, out of Thorin's line of sight. She leaped to her feet without realizing, and when the crowd cried out, Regan did as well.

The sword had cut into Thorin's shoulder. She gripped the rail. Blood flowed down his chest and bicep.

"It's not bad," a deep voice said from behind her.

That low, gravelly voice made her glance over her shoulder. She hadn't noticed Galen arrive.

The Imperator of the House of Galen was a few years older than his gladiators, but still in fighting shape. He had a hard, muscled body, a scarred face, and an eye patch over one eye. His remaining eye was a brilliant, icy blue. His dark hair was brushed back off his imposing face, and had a few strands of gray at the temples.

"It takes more than a cut to take Thorin down," Harper said from beside her.

Regan nodded, but she gripped the railing so tightly her knuckles started to turn white. When she turned back to the fight, she saw that they were right. Thorin continued fighting like he hadn't been hurt. It didn't even slow him down.

He threw his axe, and she watched it slam into

the large shield of one of his opponents. The shield cracked down the middle. The crowd went wild, and as she saw Thorin scoop up his axe and turn to attack again, she felt the energy of the fight fill her. A part of her was excited. By the cheering crowd, by the primal fighting, by Thorin's focus and prowess.

She understood why places like the Kor Magna Arena existed. Why fights like this appealed to the crowd and drew spectators from all over the galaxy. For the duration of the fight, everyone in the stands could be connected to the wild, primal part of their nature. As a scientist, she knew it existed. The fight spoke to the parts of a person that had been honed in the past. The fight-or-flight instinct every creature had.

For the duration of the fight, every person could forget about the mundane and stressful parts of their lives, and just focus on the raw battle of survival.

With a final clash of metal on metal, the fight was over.

As the announcers cried out the name of the House of Galen, the crowd was on its feet, cheering. Regan watched as medical teams rushed forward to collect the injured and writhing Thraxian gladiators from the sand.

Harper leaned forward. "Maybe Thorin's injury was worse than we thought."

Regan saw Thorin was bleeding badly. His entire chest was covered with blood. Worried, she jumped up. "We need to help him."

Harper shot her a look. "Galen's got an entire medical team—"

But Regan was already hurrying to get to the entrance to the tunnels to meet the winning gladiators.

She'd been playing around with the fantastic med gel the Medical team used, trying to enhance its properties. It could help Thorin.

And, for some reason, she wouldn't believe Thorin was all right until she saw it with her own eyes.

Chapter Two

Thorin's blood was pumping thickly. He was hot, sweaty, and his shoulder and chest were stinging like the bite of a draskan bloodsucker. "I need an ale. A big, frothy one."

"You need to get to Medical," Raiden said from behind him.

"For this?" Thorin waved at his shoulder wound. "It's nothing."

He'd had worse. Much worse. And even though the injury was stinging, it was worth it for the dark satisfaction of having taken down those bastard Thraxians.

He thought of how big the Thraxians were, and how small their prey usually was. He thought of that young man they'd forced into the arena. Thorin knew that Raiden and Galen would have already marked the boy for rescue. They'd get him out of there. Then the image of a delicate face and hair like sunshine instantly appeared in his head.

As his gut cramped, he looked down at his hands. He was just as big as the Thraxians. He had a big body that was covered in scars, and hiding secrets he preferred to keep buried. He looked at his callused hands and shook his head. He had no right to be thinking about pretty, soft females.

As they neared the tunnel leading into the depths of the arena, shouts echoed from the stands above them.

"Raiden! You're the best."

"I'm all yours, Kace!"

"Thorin, I'll suck your big cock any day!"

Thorin grinned, but didn't bother looking up. The flutterers were out in full force, high from the fight. They were women—and a few men—who liked rough sex with rough gladiators. He'd always admired their straightforward way of stating their desires. They wanted sex, nothing more, and nothing less. He'd taken more than a few of them up on their offers over the years, tending to pick the taller, stronger ones.

They stepped into the tunnel and the noise level decreased. Instantly, he saw Harper striding toward them. Raiden pushed forward to meet his woman.

The gladiator grabbed the woman around the waist, lifted her up so her legs wrapped around his hips, and planted a huge kiss on her mouth. She was laughing.

Thorin shook his head. Big, bad Raiden gone over a woman. Thorin had never thought he'd see the day. But he was happy as hell for his friend. Raiden had lost everything—even his entire planet—and now, when he looked at this small, strong human woman, he looked like he held everything right there between his hands.

For a second, Thorin wondered what that felt

like. Then he turned his head and saw *her*. Regan.

She was hovering back a few steps. She was small, but had a body filled with generous curves. She'd put on some weight over the last few weeks, the hollow look to her cheeks filling out. Still, they were so small, these human females of Earth.

Regan finally moved toward him, and Thorin felt every muscle in his body tense.

"Are you all right?" she asked.

He blinked. After a fight, everyone wanted to congratulate him, or relive parts of the battle. No one ever asked if he was okay.

He dredged up a smile, even though it felt a bit brittle. "Sure thing, sweetness."

"Your shoulder?" Her gaze lingered on the blood and gore staining his chest. "It looks bad."

He could already feel his body healing the wound. "It's fine."

Regan leaned closer, pressing one slim finger against his skin. "It's not fine. It's still bleeding." She reached out, her small hand wrapping around his. For a second, he was caught by her pale skin against his darker skin. Her tiny hand against his huge one.

"Come on. I'll clean it up for you."

Thorin wasn't sure how to pull away from her without hurting her. "I'll get down to Medical—"

She shook her head. "I've been working with the med gel they use down there. I think I've enhanced its healing capabilities. The stuff was already amazing, better than anything we had on Earth, but I think my new version is even better."

He wasn't sure why, but he let her drag him along the tunnels and through the large double doors into the House of Galen. She pulled him down the corridor, her stride determined, and into the small room that he knew Galen had allocated for her personal use.

Thorin looked around the tight space, seeing that she'd turned the place into a science lab. A bench against the wall was filled with various glass canisters and vials. She had an old, chunky info pad and some other tech he guessed she'd borrowed off people. On the ledge under the only window, several different plants were stacked neatly in small pots. Some had green foliage, others had leaves of bright red, and a few were little more than wilted stalks. Something was blooming, its lush, sweet scent filling the space and flooding his enhanced senses. His species, the Sirrush, had very good vision, hearing, and sense of smell. They usually avoided blooming plants and perfumes.

She waved him toward a chair, and he sat down.

"What have you been doing in here?" he asked.

She shrugged a shoulder, filling a bowl with water from the small sink in the corner. "I needed to find something to keep myself busy. I'm not a fighter like Harper. I had to do something to be useful."

He straightened. "Galen offering you a place to stay isn't dependent on how much value you bring."

"I know. But I can't just sit around doing nothing." Shadows moved through her eyes. "I was a botanist back on Earth. I specialize in studying plants and their healing properties."

That explained the many plants. He pulled in a breath, but instead of scenting the plants, he smelled only Regan. She had a softer, sweeter scent.

"Well, if you can get the plants around here looking healthy, that would be great. Usually they all look scraggly."

She made a sound. "That's because no one waters them."

He shrugged. Most of the time, he didn't even notice the plants.

"I've rescued a few." She moved closer, holding a damp cloth. She started wiping away the blood on his shoulder. "I watched you take down all the Thraxians."

Thorin fought the urge to hunch his shoulders. Having her so close, touching him, was disconcerting. "It's my job to take the crud-spawn bastards down. Not the first time, and it won't be the last."

Color filled her cheeks. "Right. You would've done it anyway." Her voice lowered to a whisper. "But thank you."

He was a sandsucker for lying to her. He had done it for her.

Regan finished washing the blood off his chest and shoulder. Then she grabbed a small pot of blue med gel. She dipped her fingers into the luminous gel, then started rubbing it onto his skin.

"Your rate of healing is amazing." She leaned so close to him that he felt the puff of her breath on his skin. She was practically straddling one of his legs.

Thorin curled his hands around the arms of the chair. His breathing was coming a little faster and, drak, his cock swelled.

All he could smell was her. This delicate, lovely woman was not for him. She smelled sweet and he smelled like blood and sweat. He was a big, rough brute. He'd done things that would give her nightmares. He *was* a nightmare.

"Yes." She brushed his shoulder. "The gel's working."

He looked down and saw she was right. The gel was working faster than he'd ever seen before. Usually, it took several hours for the gel to seal a wound like this. But he could see the raw edges of the wound healing before his eyes.

"That's amazing." He looked up at her. "You need to tell Galen. He'll want to know about this."

The smile she shot him was blinding. It made his hard cock press painfully against his leather trousers.

Thorin stood abruptly. "I've got to go."

She took a step back, startled. She lifted her hand, then let it drop back to her side. "Oh, right. You'll want to go and celebrate your win. I hear the parties can get pretty wild."

He gave her a stiff nod, and then headed for the door. "Thanks for the gel." He needed some space. He needed to get away from this woman who somehow twisted him up in knots without even trying.

"You deserved to win," she said quietly. "You were magnificent. I mean...out there, fighting, you were magnificent."

Thorin stopped in the doorway. No one in his entire life had ever called him magnificent. Weapon, brute, beast, warrior...never magnificent. He wanted to turn back and look at her, hell, he wanted to turn and grab her.

Instead, he curled his fingers against his palms until his knuckles turned white. He walked out, not letting himself look back at the small woman from Earth who turned him to mush.

***

Early the next morning, Regan could barely contain her excitement.

She was heading to the Kor Magna Markets. She finished straightening the covers on her bed in the room that was now her bedroom. She was grateful to have this room and her lab. She knew that new gladiatorial recruits spent their first few days in cells before they earned the privilege of the dormitories. Only the high-level gladiators had their own rooms.

Focus on the markets, Regan. She'd heard all about the amazing underground markets from Harper. She needed a few things for her lab, and she was looking forward to taking a look around.

Instead of the bland, loose-fitting trousers and shirt she'd been wearing since she got there, she was wearing a dress Harper had found for her.

Regan moved, the soft folds of the blue fabric swishing around her knees. It left one shoulder bare and knotted over her right shoulder. It was pretty, and for the first time in a very long time, she felt pretty.

"And you need to wear this." Harper entered the room, holding out a cloak. "It's got the logo of the House of Galen on it. It'll offer some protection. There are some parts of Kor Magna that can get a little...rowdy."

Regan took the gray cloak, her hands clenching on the fabric. As she stared at the logo of a helmeted gladiator head in profile, her throat tightened. "Someone might try to...snatch us?" God, what if the Thraxians came after her again?

Harper gripped her shoulder. "Don't worry. Raiden and Thorin are coming with us."

Most likely because Raiden wouldn't stay away from Harper, let alone allow her out of his sight. The way the big, tattooed gladiator watched Harper made Regan shiver.

Then her thoughts turned to Thorin. To those quiet moments in her lab, her stroking gel over his skin. She couldn't imagine a man so full of life looking at her like Raiden looked at Harper. Thorin burned with energy and wasn't afraid of anything. Regan knew she was ordinary.

She'd spent her life dating nice guys. She'd had nice conversations, nice dates, and nice sex. Something told her that Thorin didn't have nice sex. She'd heard rumors of him having sex with women right after a fight.

No, he'd have hot, dirty sex…

"Regan? Hey, where did you go?" Harper snapped her fingers in front of Regan's face.

"Sorry." She straightened. "I'm ready."

There was a noise in the doorway.

"Ready?" Raiden asked.

"Yes," Harper replied, moving to his side.

Regan looked up and saw Thorin give her a slow nod.

Soon they were moving through the tunnels, heading toward the exit that would lead them to the heart of Kor Magna city.

She found herself walking beside Thorin. "How's your shoulder?"

"All healed."

When he didn't say anything else, she sighed. Okay, she might be fascinated by the big man, but clearly he didn't return her interest.

When they reached an arched entrance, Raiden nodded at the guards, and they stepped out into the sunlight.

Regan gasped. Ahead, sleek, gleaming buildings covered in bright lights rose up, spearing into the sky. People crowded the streets, a flurry of noise and color, and in the distance, she could see a giant fountain spurting water. Carthago was a desert planet, so she knew the fountain was an extravagance.

A giant, billboard-type sign nearby blinked and flashed. It was covered in an alien language, but from the images of grinning, beautiful, scantily-clad females, she could guess what it was advertising.

"Welcome to the Kor Magna District," Harper said.

"It reminds me of the Las Vegas Strip," Regan said.

"It's the Strip on steroids. Bigger, more alien, more temptations on offer. Most locals avoid it like the plague. Gambling, fighting, prostitution, drugs—" Harper shook her head. "You name it, you can find it in the District. They come for the arena fights and stay for all the vices."

Raiden and Thorin were leading them away from the bright lights. A few blocks off the main road of the District, the buildings evolved into simple, two-story affairs, made from the same cream stone as the arena.

"But the market isn't attached to the District?" Regan asked.

Harper shook her head. "This market is used by the locals. It provides all the goods the gladiators and regular citizens need." She shot Regan a rueful smile. "Still plenty of temptations around, though."

They moved into an alley, and headed toward a giant, circular hole in the ground. As they got closer, she saw a huge spiral ramp carved into the walls, disappearing downward into a brightly lit chamber.

"Apparently, the planet is covered in subterranean caves and sinkholes like this one," Harper told her.

A short while later, the ramp leveled out, and

they stepped out into a cavernous underground space filled with rows of stalls and crowds of people.

Regan smiled. It was almost medieval. Light filtered in from aboveground, augmented by orange lamps attached to the walls. The walls were a beautiful, smooth rock, the color of the arena sand. She studied the throng. People were dressed in everything from slick jumpsuits to billowing robes, laughing, chattering, and negotiating.

She waited for the press of people and noise to bother her, but instead, the hubbub and bustle of the market seemed normal. She could almost imagine she was back at the farmers' market that she liked to frequent on Earth.

"Come on," Thorin said, nudging her along.

As they moved along, Regan stopped to look at every stall. It looked like you could get everything here: fruits, vegetables, clothing, jewelry, and crafts. She took in large boxes filled to the brim with alien fruits and vegetables of all shapes and sizes. There were weapons, beautiful pieces of armor and helmets, different liniments and lotions for the gladiators. She paused to look thoughtfully at one table filled with jars and tubes. Maybe, if she perfected her own lotions and things, she could do something like this and sell some goods here?

The next stall was filled with food. Delicate cakes and pastries, small lumps of...well, she wasn't quite sure. Maybe they were cookies. She desperately wanted to try something, but was equally worried it might make her sick.

"*Grezzo.*" Thorin leaned forward and showed a small token to the stall owner. It was engraved with the House of Galen logo. Then he turned and held out a small, dark square to Regan. "Here. Try this."

Regan sniffed the treat, then gingerly nibbled the edge of the square. Flavor exploded in her mouth and she moaned, before shoving the remainder in. "Oh my God, Thorin. This tastes almost like chocolate. One of my most favorite things." She looked up.

He had a strange look on his face and was watching her lips.

"Have I got it on my mouth?" She swiped the back of her hand across her jaw.

He shook his head. "You like the *grezzo?*"

"I love it." She smiled. "Thank you. No woman should be abducted and taken halfway across the galaxy, and then have to live without chocolate."

He gave her a long look and then pushed ahead, catching up with Raiden and Harper.

Letting out a gusty sigh, Regan turned her attention back to the stalls. It seemed that no matter how hard she tried, she couldn't quite get things right with Thorin. Most of the time he watched her like a weapon that was about to explode in his face.

She paused at a stall selling fabulously intricate leather harnesses and armor for the arena. The workmanship was incredible. They also had some beautiful jewelry, and her gaze fell on a strip of leather with sparkly green stones dotted along it.

"Hello." Somebody touched her shoulder.

She spun and looked up at the giant man standing beside her. He looked humanoid, with heavy features and long brown hair, but then she saw two small horns coming out of the top of his head.

"You're a pretty little thing." His dark eyes skated over her, lingering on her breasts.

Regan managed a tight smile. "Have a nice day." She turned away, trying to spot the others. God, where were they?

As she stepped away, something held her back. She glanced over her shoulder and saw the man's hand was fisted in the back of her dress.

"Don't run off, little thing. I like the look of you." His hand slid down her side, cupping her hip.

Regan felt a brush of fear, but even stronger than that was a surge of anger. She was sick of people thinking they could grab her, lock her up, and take away her choices.

She'd vowed in that Thraxian cell that if she ever got out, she'd never be a slave again.

She lifted her hands and shoved against his chest. "Get your hands off me."

He didn't budge, but the shock on his face was almost comical.

Then it morphed into a scowl and he yanked on her dress, making her stumble. "No one says no to Grash."

Chapter Three

Regan gathered herself, ready to launch herself at the man. Suddenly, a big body brushed past her, and shoved the man away.

"Leave her alone."

Thorin's voice was as deep and icy as a frozen river.

Regan felt goose bumps rise on her skin. "Thorin—"

Her attacker's eyes widened and he held his hands up. "Sorry, sorry."

"You do not touch what isn't yours." Thorin wrapped an arm around Regan's waist.

"Sorry. I didn't realize she was yours. I didn't realize she belonged to the House of Galen." The man backed away.

Thorin stared at him, until the man turned and hurried off into the crowd. Then he looked down at her. "You shouldn't have wandered off. It's easy to get lost in the maze of tunnels down here."

She bristled. "I didn't ask that idiot to grab me."

"I know that. But the market isn't always safe. You need to be careful."

Regan tucked a strand of hair back behind her ear. He had a point. This wasn't her world, and she was still learning to navigate it. He shifted against her, and the warmth radiating off his big body was distracting. "I would have dealt with him, but thanks."

"Dealt with him?" Thorin's voice dropped. "He was twice your size, Regan."

"I'm not stupid, Thorin. And you don't require brawn to deal with everything." She turned, ready to move on. She cast the pretty necklace one last look. It was lovely, but it was also a glaring reminder that she didn't have any money. She got an empty feeling in her stomach. She had nothing that was hers. Right now, she was living off the charity of Harper and the House of Galen.

She spotted Raiden and Harper ahead, and kept moving. She'd have to find a way to support herself. But what was she going to do? She wasn't a gladiator, or healer, and as far as she could see, they didn't have much need for botanists in Kor Magna.

Thorin stayed by her side. A big, silent presence.

As they walked, she spotted something that made her chest hitch. An entire stall of plants. Most of which she'd never seen before.

She slowed down, desperately wanting to look at them. God, so many were completely different from anything she'd seen on Earth. One with bright purple leaves looked fascinating, and another looked vaguely like a cactus and was covered in beautiful red flowers.

Thorin huffed out a breath. "We can stop and have a look at the stall."

ANNA HACKETT

She shot him a small smile. "You're sure?"

"Look before I change my mind."

She smiled at the tiny, wizened man running the stall and gently touched a few different leaves. The storeowner happily told her the names of each plant. The one plant with the delicate purple leaves kept drawing her gaze. It was so pretty, and she would give anything to study it.

Suddenly, a muscled arm reached past her, holding out a House of Galen token. "How much for the purple plant?"

"Thorin, no. I don't need it—"

He ignored her, paid, and took the pot from the table. He shoved it at her. "You wanted it."

It wasn't the most gracious way she'd ever been given a gift, but she took it and stroked the purple leaves. It was something that was hers. Not borrowed, or reclaimed from unused things. Hers. "Thank you."

He gave a single nod, turned her with a gentle touch at her back, and urged her onward.

Regan snuck glances up at his face. It was a tough face that no one would accuse of being handsome. But she liked it. It had character.

She wanted him. She wanted this man. He might be big and strong, but he'd only ever done things to help her and make her feel safe. Some things, like buying her a plant, she felt he was doing against his better judgment. The man had a soft center he refused to expose, and Regan desperately wanted to see more of it.

But it was clear he didn't feel the same way. She

28

knew that he was a fierce warrior of the arena and he had his choice of women. Hell, she'd seen the way women threw themselves at the gladiators. She'd heard wild stories of some of the after-parties. She heard some pretty crazy stories about Thorin specifically, and what he liked.

Feeling a little depressed, she continued along beside him, halfheartedly glancing at stalls as they moved into some crowded side tunnels. Regan glanced up, looking ahead to where they were going, and saw a flash of red hair in the throng of people.

Her heart clenched. She hadn't seen any red hair since she'd arrived on the planet. Her cousin Rory had red hair. Riotous curls the woman was always cursing. Almost as much as her fair skin and freckles. Regan's hand clenched on the plant pot.

She searched again for that flash of red. *There.* The woman was turned away from her, but...Regan frowned. There was something about the way the woman held herself, the way she walked...

Without thinking, Regan pushed through the crowd to try and get a better look.

It was definitely a woman. With an athletic stride and a stubborn tilt to her chin. Just like Regan's mixed-martial-arts-trained cousin. Regan's chest was so tight she felt like she couldn't breathe.

Regan kept moving, willing the woman to turn around so she could see her face. Regan couldn't be sure.

"Rory!" she shouted.

Even though she was far away, the woman turned toward Regan's shout. Regan strained, trying to see...but before she could do anything else, the tall aliens flanking the redhead grabbed her and dragged her away. The crowd swallowed them.

Regan's heart was beating so hard it hurt. Even if she could get through the crowd, she'd never reach them in time. Had it been Rory? She was pretty sure.

Then she glanced at her surroundings, and realized that in her mad rush to see the woman, she'd lost Thorin.

And ahead of her, a gang of men were lounging against the rock wall, watching her. She glanced back. She couldn't see Thorin, Harper, or Raiden anywhere.

She straightened her shoulders and backed away. It was all in the attitude, right? Don't show your fear, look like you belonged.

She'd barely taken two steps, when a man walked in front of her, blocking her way.

"Leaving so soon?" he said.

He was, of course, bigger and taller than her, and looked humanoid, with a pattern of dark rosettes over his skin. "Yes. My friends will be looking for me."

He reached out and grabbed her arm roughly. "I think it's time to make some new friends."

As he pulled her forward, her plant fell from her hands and hit the hard-packed dirt. She cried out, and tried to yank away, her cloak flaring out around her body.

One of the man's friends gasped. "Hey, Dolan, she's wearing a House of Galen cloak."

The man, Dolan, hesitated. He lifted his head, looking around. "I don't see anyone with her." His dark gaze dropped back to Regan. "Give me your token."

"I don't have one."

"Coins, then."

"I don't have any of those either. And even if I did, I wouldn't give them to you." She yanked her arm.

He pulled her forward, and they started a tug-of-war. The muscles in Regan's arms started to burn.

"Just leave me the hell alone." She shoved her hands against his chest.

All of a sudden, the man released her and backed away. His eyes widened, and he raised his hands. Regan blinked slowly. Well. That was more like it.

And that's when she felt a big body behind her. She wasn't the one scaring her assailant.

"I should rip your head off." A menacing growl.

Okay, she'd thought Thorin sounded scary before, but now he sounded downright deadly.

"We're out of here, Thorin," another man said. "Sorry. I warned Dolan not to touch her."

Thorin's gaze swung to Dolan. "You knew she was House of Galen, and you still touched her?"

Dolan's mouth opened and closed like a fish.

Thorin took a threatening step forward. "I see you anywhere near her again, I will rip your arms and legs off."

Then Thorin turned, grabbed Regan's arm, and tugged her into the crowd.

He was silent but she felt his anger pulsing off him.

"Thorin, wait," she cried out.

He stopped and scooped up something. Her plant. It was slightly battered, but still in its pot. He shoved it at her. "You don't wander off—"

"I know. You can be angry at me later." She reached out and grabbed his thick forearm with her free hand. "Thorin, I saw Rory! My cousin. She was alive and right here! I'm sure—" Regan ran out of breath.

"Calm down." Thorin's hand moved up to her shoulder. "Tell me again."

"I saw Rory. She has red hair, which I haven't seen much around here."

Thorin nodded. "It's rare."

Her fingers dug into his skin. "I saw my cousin. Some aliens were herding her across the market."

"You're sure?"

"It was only a quick glimpse, but it was her."

"Okay." He smoothed a hand down her arm. "Come on. Let's find the others."

"You'll help me?" Regan asked. "You'll help me rescue her, just like you and Harper rescued me?"

His big chest rose and fell. He touched her face. "Yes, Regan. I'll help you."

***

Thorin sat in their living area, watching as Regan paced. Her steps were jerky, without her usual grace. On a nearby couch, Harper sat watching her with concern on her face.

"It was Rory," Regan insisted.

From behind Harper, Raiden nodded. He lifted a red-and-gray wall hanging aside, uncovering a wall filled with screens and images taped to the brick.

Regan paused to look at the information. She didn't look surprised, so Thorin figured Harper had told her friend about the House of Galen's extracurricular rescue activities.

"Okay," Raiden said. "Can you describe the aliens who were with her?"

Regan's brow scrunched. "Humanoid. Nondescript. They were too far away for me to see any details. And I was paying more attention to her."

"You're a scholar, Regan. A scientist," Thorin said. "You notice things. Try harder."

She huffed out a breath, putting her hands on her hips. "They were tall." She eyed Thorin. "But not as big as you. They had slimmer builds."

"Come and look at these images." Raiden waved at the wall. "See if any look familiar."

Regan scanned the wall, lines bracketing her mouth. She shook her head.

Galen was leaning against the wall, a scowl on his face. "Okay, I'll do what I can with what we have. I'll put out feelers to my contacts."

"Perhaps we should talk to Zhim," Thorin suggested.

Galen grimaced. "I'd prefer not to."

Thorin understood. The local information merchant was intelligent, arrogant, and annoying. But aside from his aggravating personality, he kept his fingers on the pulse of information in Kor Magna. He was also expensive and difficult to work with.

"No one's offered an Earth female for sale...that I know of." Galen's look turned sour. "And I'm getting a reputation for collecting them."

"That's it?" Regan threw her arms out. "We put out feelers again and we wait?"

"For now." Galen's tone deepened. "In the meantime, we have a fight to prepare for. I need my gladiators to train, prepare, and get some rest before tomorrow."

Regan stared at him for a minute, before her gaze swung back to Thorin's. She was biting her lip.

"Galen's right," Thorin said.

She turned and strode from the room.

Harper stood, ready to follow her.

Thorin shook his head. "I'll go."

When he got out into the stone-lined corridor, it was empty. She couldn't have made it to her lab that quickly. He knew exactly where she'd go. If she wasn't working, it was her favorite spot, and he'd seen her there numerous times during his training.

He stepped out onto the balcony. As he'd guessed, she was curled in a ball on a chair overlooking the empty training arena below. The space was ringed with plants and he could see they were already looking healthier, so he guessed that Regan was taking care of them.

"You okay?" He moved toward the railing.

She pressed her cheek to her knee. "We should do more. We should search—"

"It's a big arena, and an even bigger city." His gaze tracked over the arena walls to the tops of the District's towering spires. "And one of the rules of this place is to never show interest in something. That just raises its price, and people will use that against you."

She squeezed her eyes shut, her lashes dark against her pale cheeks. "I'm worried she's being hurt, beaten..." Regan's voice drifted off.

"Like you were." He knew his voice was harsh, clipped. His hands curled around the stone railing, and he felt rage pounding inside him. How could the Thraxians beat a small, soft woman like Regan?

She looked up, then she nodded. "But I got out. I'm safe. Rory isn't." A shaky breath. "Sometimes I have nightmares."

He saw the old horror swimming in her eyes. A single tear tracked down her cheek. He wanted to touch her, but he was afraid that with his giant, rough hands that he'd just make it worse. He knew nothing of comforting someone. He only knew fighting and killing.

She lifted a hand and brushed the tear away. "You must think I'm weak."

"No." He dropped down into the chair beside her.

"The opposite. I think you're a survivor. I think you're very strong."

She tilted her head. "Why?"

"When you're taken from everything you know and care about, when you are dumped somewhere against your will, the easiest thing to do is to give up."

She made a small sound, her hand pressing down on top of his.

He hurried on before she could ask any questions he didn't want to answer. "Another option is that you grow hard. You stop caring and you fight solely for yourself." He looked her in the eyes. "But I've seen you smile. I've seen the way you care for Harper."

Regan's breath hitched. "I was so alone for so long...sometimes I wanted to give up."

"But you didn't, and you aren't alone anymore." He wasn't sure if she moved first or he did, but the next thing he knew, her curvy, little body was curled up in his lap. She burrowed into him, and Thorin held on to her.

"I have to save Rory," she whispered. "I'll do *anything* to save her. I can't leave her all alone."

Regan began to cry quietly and he stroked her back, not sure if he was comforting her or himself. He was careful not to hold her too tight. He didn't want to hurt her.

Since he'd been sold into slavery, Thorin had used the arena and the fights to block out the pain of his past. To forget he'd been used, turned into a weapon, and then thrown out.

To forget the dark heart of what beat inside him.

Every fight, every blow, each drop of blood he shed...it all helped him forget the past. He'd pieced a life together here in the arena, and he liked it. The adoration of the crowd, the willing women, the friends he'd made.

But for the first time in a long time, he wanted to take care of someone else. He wanted to protect the small woman in his arms.

And Thorin vowed he would. He'd help her save her friend, and give her everything she deserved...and that definitely didn't include him.

Chapter Four

If anyone found out what she was doing, she was going to be in big trouble.

Regan forced herself to walk calmly, her hands clasped in front of her. She was walking two steps behind the Hermia healers, who were heading out of the House of Galen.

If Harper found out that Regan had snuck out...

God, if Thorin found out...

Regan pulled in a calming breath. She wasn't going to go far, or leave the network of tunnels beneath the arena. She'd thought this all through. Yes, it was risky, but she had a plan, and a small dagger stashed in her pocket for protection. But she had no intention of engaging anyone. She pulled her sand-colored cloak around her, a hood up and covering her face.

She had to do this. For Rory.

Before she knew it, they'd passed the guards standing at the House of Galen doors, and they were out in the tunnels. She lifted her chin and broke away from the healers. She'd memorized a map of the tunnels, the location of all the gladiator houses, the area where the arena workers lived. There was practically an entire city under the arena.

She was determined to find out any information she could on where Rory might be. Rory was tough and practical, and, like Harper, she was trained to fight. Not that she'd worked in security, but she'd often sparred with Harper in the space station gym. But Regan knew what the slavers could do to people, grind you down until you felt like an animal.

It didn't matter how strong you were. In fact, strength could be worse...something they felt compelled to break. The Thraxians had done everything they could to break her down, until all that was left was fear.

Regan stumbled to a stop. She pressed a palm against the smooth stone wall, breathing deep. She wasn't afraid anymore, and she was going to find Rory.

The sensible place to start was with the Thraxians. They were the ones who'd abducted Rory in the first place. The rumor they'd heard was that the Thraxians had moved her and—Regan's stomach clenched—potentially sold her to someone local.

Regan forced herself to get closer to the House of Thrax. As she neared the huge double doors, her pulse quickened. Light reflected off the copper-colored metal and the House of Thrax logo in the center—a head with a set of horns.

She kept her gaze down, careful not to make eye

contact with the Thraxian guards flanking the doors.

As she strolled past, the doors opened. She tensed, but it was only a group of off-duty workers who exited. They were huddled together, chatting. She'd spent enough time inside to know that the workers were a mix of different species, who did jobs like cleaning and cooking for their Thraxian masters.

The workers moved off, and Regan fell in behind them. She tried to look like she was minding her own business, but strained to hear what they were talking about.

"Let's head to the Sword and Shield. I need an ale and a game of *bach*."

"You're terrible at *bach*. You always lose everything."

As the group continued to tease their friend for not playing the game of *bach* very well, Regan followed them. They were going to a bar. That was good. She could blend in, and maybe they'd relax and talk about what was going on inside the House of Thrax.

They moved to a busier part of the tunnels. Regan saw people with small tables selling various trinkets and small goods. A few enterprising children in grubby clothes were running a shell game with small cups and colored stones.

The workers moved through an arched doorway. Above it, was a stone carved with the image of a rectangular shield with a sword crossing it. From inside, Regan could hear music and talking. She followed them inside.

When she got a good look at the bar, she hesitated. The place was...rough. There was a long, carved-stone bar at the rear of the large room, with a grizzled bartender filling glasses with brown liquid. Off to the left were tables and chairs filled with lots of different species, and on the right-hand side were what appeared to be various gaming tables. The place smelled of unwashed bodies and alcohol.

She moved toward the bar, waiting to see where the House of Thrax workers would sit. She let her gaze drift over the crowd. She saw some men scuffling in a corner, landing hard punches. She winced. She heard some women laughing out loud, as they played a game with a holographic tower in the center of their table.

When she saw the workers sit at a round table, she moved over and found a free chair not far away. She turned her back to them, but listened intently.

As she predicted, they got drinks and started to relax. They also started to moan about working for the House of Thrax.

"Always orders," one woman grumbled. "Never a kind word."

"They're Thraxian," a man said. "If you wanted kind, you should have gone elsewhere. As long as they pay, I don't care about their manners."

"Just be happy you're not on the other side of their cages," another man said darkly.

Regan pressed her hands to her table. *Come on.*

Talk about Rory.

Someone stopped by her table. "You sit here, you buy a drink."

She looked up. It was the rough bartender. "Ah…okay. I'll have whatever's good." She had one tiny coin that Harper had given her.

The bartender's yellow-brown gaze narrowed. "Nothing's good." He stomped off.

Regan blew out a breath, and tuned back in to the workers' conversation behind her. Comments about the Thraxians' latest auction caught her ear.

"Heard they got a pretty penny for their latest pet. Finally sold her off."

"Maybe she's better off somewhere else."

"I heard the Thraxian imperator was glad to get rid of this one. She was trouble. A fighter."

Regan strained to hear more.

"I think they just wanted to avoid any more confrontation with the House of Galen."

Suddenly, a glass was slammed down on the table, spilling some frothy ale over the side.

"Ale," the bartender growled at her. She pulled out her coin and handed it to him. He stomped away.

Regan lifted the drink and took a sip. Then she spluttered. It wasn't like any beer she'd ever had. She tried not to cough, her eyes watering. The damn stuff nearly took her head off. *Jeez.*

The workers behind her were now talking about something else, gossiping about some man and woman who couldn't keep their hands off each other.

Regan tapped the table. They had to have been talking about Rory. Okay, she'd been sold and she wasn't with the Thraxians. At least she had something to work with, now.

Suddenly, another big body stopped by her table and Rory looked up again. Way up. The alien towered over her. He had dark, iridescent skin that gleamed under the lights, making her think of sunlight on a black pearl. "We want you to come and play *bach* with us."

She smiled. "No, thank you. I'm waiting for a friend."

"I wasn't asking."

Regan barely stopped herself from rolling her eyes. What was it with the males on this planet? One look at her, and they just thought they could boss her around. She lifted her drink and stood. "I said no, thank you—"

That's when her foot collided with the edge of the table and she tipped forward. Her drink splashed over the alien's chest.

Uh, oh. "I'm so sorry—"

The alien spluttered, tugging at his wet shirt. "That was a grave insult."

It was? "I said I was sorry. I didn't intend to—"

"Baront, this female disgraced you by throwing her drink at you." Another alien appeared, staring at his friend's wet chest in horror. "A grave insult."

"It was an accident." She threw her hand out and accidentally smacked someone walking past. She turned and saw another alien. This one was covered in a long, shaggy fur.

43

"Watch yourself," the alien barked.

Regan stepped back and knocked into another scaled alien. This one stumbled into the one she'd splashed with her drink.

Before she could say anything else, Baront shoved the scaled alien who'd bumped him. The scaled alien let out an angry hiss and shoved back.

In a blink, a fight broke out.

As fists flew, Regan ducked. Someone bumped into her, and as she stumbled, she saw a table sail past her head.

Oh, God. She dropped to her hands and knees. As she scrambled toward another table, she heard the thud of kicks and punches, and saw bodies hitting the floor.

Chairs scraped, and it looked like everyone was joining the fight.

Oh, hell. Regan scooted under another table. *What now, Regan?*

***

Thorin pushed himself harder, running through the obstacle course set up in the training arena.

He pumped his arms and leaped over some stacked stones. He raced across some logs, then jumped into the air, swinging his axe over his head.

The axe slammed into the target—a sack filled with sand.

He stopped, his lungs heaving, and rested the head of his axe on the ground.

"That's the twentieth time you've been through

the course." Raiden appeared beside him. "You're pushing yourself pretty hard today."

Thorin grunted and swung his axe up over his shoulder.

"Why?" Raiden set his hands on his hips, the tattoos on his arms flexing with his muscles.

"No reason."

His friend didn't look convinced. Thorin wasn't going to admit that he was trying to get the feel of Regan out of his head. If he was tired enough and sore enough, maybe he'd stop thinking about her.

"We still on for the mission for tonight?" Thorin asked. He sure hoped they were. He needed the action to keep him busy.

Raiden nodded. "A worker in the House of Gorm'lah will smuggle the two underage slaves out. We'll meet them and transport them to the spaceport. Galen's arranged berths for them on a freighter."

Thorin felt a flood of satisfaction. This was the true work he and the other gladiators did. They fought in the arena, seemingly for the glory and prestige, but underneath it all, they helped smuggle the abducted, the injured, the slaves, and the smaller, weaker gladiators out of the arena.

It was then he spotted a young kid hovering in the first row of seats of the training arena. The boy looked antsy. Thorin frowned. It was Dash. He was an arena rat—orphan kids that lived and worked around the arena—who had helped get a message to Harper once about Regan. Now, they paid the boy to run errands.

ANNA HACKETT

"What's Dash doing here?" Thorin said.

Raiden frowned. "He looks twitchy."

Together, they walked over to the boy. "Dash," Thorin greeted him.

The young boy wiped a hand across his mouth. "Your female's in trouble. The Earth woman."

Thorin glanced over his shoulder, looking at where Harper was training on the other side of the arena. She was working with some new recruits.

Raiden shook his head. "Harper's right here."

Dash shook his head, his dark hair flying. "No, not your woman. Thorin's."

Thorin straightened. "Regan?" Some unfamiliar emotion rushed through him, leaving his chest tight. "What's happened to her? Where is she?"

"Heard from a bartender at a dive bar in the lower levels where the arena workers go. The Shield and Sword."

Thorin resisted the urge to grab the boy. "I've heard of it."

"He said she's there. She started a fight."

Thorin cursed. He spun, striding toward the tunnels. What the hell was Regan doing out of the House of Galen alone? Drak, what was she doing in a bar, starting a fight?

"Lore? Nero? Need you," Raiden called out. "Bring a weapon."

As the two big gladiators headed over, Harper spotted them.

She jogged across the arena. "What's wrong?"

Thorin forced himself to pause. His hands flexed. He needed to get to Regan.

46

"Regan went out for a wander." Raiden reached up, sliding his short sword into the scabbard on his back.

"I'm coming," Harper said grimly.

Raiden gripped her shoulder. "You have recruits to train. Take care of them, and we'll bring her back safely."

Harper's jaw tightened, and she looked like she wanted to argue. Then she looked at Thorin.

He nodded at her. "I'll find her."

"Go," Harper said.

Thorin stepped into the tunnel, the cooler air swirling around him. Anger was rising. If anyone hurt her…

"Can you keep your cool, or do I have to lock you down?"

Thorin didn't even look at Raiden. "I'm cool."

"What's she doing out of the House of Galen?" Lore asked.

Thorin growled. "I plan to find out."

It didn't take long for them to reach the Shield and Sword. Before they reached the doorway, Thorin heard the sounds of brawling. A body came flying out of the door. The alien man hit the stone floor and skidded, letting out a loud groan.

Thorin stepped over the body and entered the bar. Raiden, Lore, and Nero were right behind him.

He searched the gloom, but he couldn't see her. There were bodies everywhere—people fighting, others cowering behind tables and chairs. A chair flew over the bar, smashing bottles on a shelf.

The bartender, a grizzled looking man, barely

reacted. He was polishing glasses at the end of the bar.

Thorin hefted his axe. Those bar patrons closest to the door noticed the four of them had entered. A few stopped fighting, shifting away. Slowly, most of the room stilled. They sensed that there were bigger predators in the room.

Another sweep of the room, and Thorin spotted Regan. She was huddled under a table in the center of the room, wrapped in a sand-colored cloak.

There were still two aliens fighting beside her. One shoved the other and they crashed into Regan's table, tipping it over.

When a giant Taazon spotted her, he grabbed her ankle and yanked her out into the open.

A muscle in Thorin's jaw ticked. He strode forward.

"Thorin, don't kill anyone," Raiden said dryly.

Thorin watched as Regan kicked the Taazon. The man laughed.

After two more strides, Thorin lifted his axe and brought it down.

The axe skimmed the Taazon's body and embedded into the edge of his boot, pinning him to the floor. Thorin had missed the man's body parts by a whisper.

"The woman is mine," Thorin said darkly.

The Taazon stared up at Thorin, his face a mask of terror. Thorin smelled the stench of urine as the man wet himself.

All around them, the bar had gone silent. He saw that Raiden and the others had fanned out, their weapons drawn.

Thorin met as many gazes as he could. "This woman has my protection. If anyone touches her, you take on me."

"You take on the House of Galen," Raiden added.

Regan pushed to her feet, dusting off her skirts. "I'm yours?" She stepped up and poked Thorin in the chest. "I'm not a thing, Thorin."

He couldn't believe she was doing this right now. "It's best you don't say anything, Regan." He was so angry right now he was afraid of what he'd do to her.

"Or what?" She poked his chest again. "I was treated like a thing for months. No more."

"I'm protecting you. It was foolish of you to come here." He grabbed her arm. He looked around and saw that everyone was watching them, wide-eyed. People were always wary of gladiators, especially Raiden and Thorin. No one had ever dared to talk to him the way that Regan was.

Even before he'd come to the arena, he'd been feared by his own people. After years of fighting in the arena, he had a fearsome reputation.

Regan wasn't afraid of him, and that was stupid of her.

"You started a fight," he said to her.

"It wasn't my fault." She pulled a face. "Mostly. It was a misunderstanding."

Tired of the argument and seeing her in this dive, he leaned down and picked her up. He tossed her over his shoulder.

She was still for a second, then she started

wriggling. He anchored her there with one big hand over her curvy butt.

Then he turned, nodded at Raiden, and strode out.

Chapter Five

Regan was mad. Madder than she'd ever been in her entire life.

She was usually a calm, sensible woman, but being tossed over Thorin's broad shoulder and carted off like a wayward child had ignited something inside her. As they strode through the tunnels, she noticed the big gladiator, Nero, grinning at her. Asshole.

Soon, they were back in the House of Galen, and, upside down, she saw Harper coming closer.

Her friend cleared her throat. "Thorin—"

"I'll deal with her." Thorin's tone was unyielding.

Harper stepped forward, about to intervene, but Raiden wrapped his arms around her and yanked her away.

Thorin kept going, striding through the living area for the high-level gladiators, and through a door. Her chest hitched. They were in his bedroom. When he slammed the door behind them, it made a loud bang.

The room was messy, his enormous bed unmade and clothes tossed on the floor. The room smelled like him—something masculine and dark. He strode over to a couch and dumped her on it. As she landed, all the air left her lungs.

"You should never have left the House of Galen." Thorin stood in front of her and crossed his big arms over his chest.

She lifted her chin. "Am I a prisoner?"

Something flickered over his face. "No. But you shouldn't have left without an escort."

She moved up onto her knees on the cushions. "You would have said no."

"Absolutely."

"I won't be held captive again."

He leaned down, big and intimidating, but she wasn't afraid. Not of Thorin.

"I am protecting you."

She looked at him, really looked at him. That's when she realized his muscles were tense, his chest heaving, and his face set in stark lines.

He'd been worried about her.

The fight went out of her. She reached up and touched his chest. "I know. You've made me feel safe. The Thraxians kept me locked up, Thorin—" her breath hitched "—I can't live like that again."

He made a sound and grabbed her, pulling her up to his chest. "Why did you go out? Don't you like it here? Do you want to leave?"

"No." She pulled back. "I needed to do something to find Rory. I followed some House of Thrax workers, hoping to overhear information."

He stared at her for a second, then, with a shake of his head, he sat down on the couch beside her. "Did you hear anything?"

She nodded. "I overheard them talking about the

Thraxians selling a woman. A fighter. I'm pretty sure they were talking about Rory."

Thorin's jaw tightened. "Sold to whom?"

"They didn't say," she whispered. "I *have* to find her." Regan pressed her hands to his chest. "Please."

His big hands wrapped around hers. "I promise we'll find her. But you have to trust me. No more running off and risking yourself."

"I didn't mean to start that bar fight—"

"I didn't think you did. But you're small, not as strong as the other people here. You don't know how to protect yourself."

She straightened. "Then you need to teach me."

"What?"

"Can you teach me how to fight and defend myself?"

For a second, Thorin looked horrified.

"It makes sense, Thorin. I'm halfway across the galaxy, on an unfamiliar, dangerous world, with no way home. I know I'll never be a gladiator, but I need to know how to protect myself."

He let out a long breath, and she could see he was caving.

"Please, Thorin."

Finally, he gave her a small nod.

She relaxed against him. "Thank you for helping me." The warmth of his big body seeped into her. He must have been training before he came to her rescue, as he was still wearing his fighting harness, and all those hard muscles of his were on display. She knew she shouldn't touch him, but her hands were itching. She reached out and stroked her fingers across his chest.

That's when she saw scales flicker on his skin, appearing in a dark blush of color.

She gasped. "Thorin."

He made a tight sound and the scales disappeared.

"Your species has scales?" she asked.

"The Sirrush do not have scales."

She frowned. "Then why—?"

"I don't want to talk about it."

There was an edge to his voice, and she swallowed. She snatched her hand back. "I'm sorry, I didn't mean to hurt you."

He grabbed her arm. "You didn't hurt me."

She shifted beside him. The scales had been beautiful. She found all of him fascinating. She stared at his large hand against her paler skin. Scars crossed his knuckles, no doubt earned in the arena. She was so attracted to him, and not just his looks, but to his strength and his urge to protect others.

Desire coiled through her. Everything about this man called to her. She wondered what those hands would feel like on other parts of her body, and at the thought, her chest tightened. Sliding along her thighs. Cupping her breasts. Slipping inside her. She felt herself go damp between her legs.

That's when Thorin pulled in a sharp breath, his face going hard.

She looked up at him and her eyes widened. "What's wrong?"

"My species...we have enhanced senses. Sight, hearing...smell."

She went stiff as metal. *Oh, my God.* He could smell her arousal.

"God." She dropped her head against his chest. "This is so embarrassing. I know you don't think of me that way. You're so big and bold, and I'm...not. You can have any woman you want—"

He gripped her chin, forcing her gaze up. "You don't think I want you?"

Her brow furrowed. "Of course you don't."

He made a noise close to a growl and grabbed her hand. He pulled it into his lap.

Regan felt the huge bulge beneath his leathers. Her eyes widened. Oh. My. God. It was his cock. Hard, huge, throbbing.

"Thorin..."

His fingers stroked her jaw. "You're pretty and delicate, but you are smart and have a resilience that is captivating. You survived captivity, beatings, everything the Thraxians threw at you. I know that in time, you would have used that clever mind of yours to free yourself. You're wrong, Regan. I want you more than I want anything else."

He cupped the back of her head and drew her forward. When his mouth met hers, something hot shot through Regan. Her lips parted and his tongue dove into her mouth. As Thorin kissed her, she felt the world tilt.

His kiss was hard and demanding. She slid her hands up, sliding over his shaved head. He had a small goatee and it scratched against her skin, adding to the thrilling sensations.

She arched into him, kissing him back. God, she wanted. She wanted to touch him and be touched. She was pressed against his wide chest, shifting until she straddled one of his hard thighs.

Suddenly he stood, dumping her out of his lap and back onto the couch. She looked up, her eyes level with the hard, enormous bulge in his tight trousers. She licked her lips, then forced herself to look up.

He looked like a conquering barbarian. His face was set in hard lines, his eyes blazing. He looked dangerous, a man on the edge.

"I vowed to protect you." His voice was strained. "I want you, but I'm not the man for you."

She frowned, her gut cramping. "What?"

"I'm dangerous, Regan. You don't know where I've come from, the things I've done, who I truly am. You deserve better."

"Don't I get a choice?" She felt her anger rising. She could see he believed every word he was saying to her. "You're a good man, Thorin, I've seen that—"

"You don't understand." He shook his head. "I was dumped here in the arena...by my brother."

She gasped. He'd been sold by his own family?

"I was already feared by my own people. I was a fierce Sirrush warrior, a weapon, and I've killed with these hands." He lifted them up. "They have no right to touch your skin. I am a killer, a gladiator who makes others bleed in the arena, a man who fucks hundreds of women whose names I never know."

His words hit her like bullets. She wrapped her arms around her middle.

"I've made a life here. A life I can live with, but this isn't the life for you."

Oh, so her gladiator was too bad for the little woman from Earth. She lifted her chin. "I think you're just surviving, Thorin, not really living."

His brows drew together. "What?"

"I think you're afraid to reach for more."

He stared at her for a second, tension pumping off his body. "I will help you learn to protect yourself. I will help you find your cousin, but that is all." He spun and walked out.

Regan slumped back against the couch and closed her eyes. Then she opened them, her jaw tightening. Her gladiator was going to find out just how strong this Earth girl could be.

***

Thorin ushered the two teenage boys through the backstreets of the city.

Ahead, Raiden, Kace, and Saff were on point, keeping a look out for any trouble. Nero and Lore were somewhere behind them, hidden in the shadows. Thorin calculated that they weren't far from the spaceport now. Just a few more blocks.

Sneaking the boys out of the House of Gorm'lah had gone off without any problems. He was almost disappointed. He would have liked a fight.

They rounded a corner and he saw the glow of the spaceport above the buildings. He glanced at the boys. They were too thin and looked tired. They'd told him they'd been abducted off a transport with their family several weeks ago and ended up being sold to the Gorm'lah.

Galen had booked them flights back to their homeworld. It must be nice to have a home to go back to.

One of the boys stumbled and Thorin grabbed his arm. Big blue eyes looked up at him, and for a second, they reminded him of Regan. The same fresh innocence.

"Thank you," the boy whispered.

"Almost there." Thorin tried to keep his voice from sounding too deep and harsh.

When the boy stumbled again, clearly out of energy, Thorin scooped him into his arms. They couldn't afford to get off schedule.

"You're so strong," the boy said. "I wish I was strong."

"You'll get strong once you're home with your family."

The boy nodded. "Do you have a family?"

Thorin shifted his gaze straight ahead. "No."

"Did you get taken from them?" The boy's voice wavered. "Like me?"

If only he knew. "Something like that. These gladiators are my family now."

"Don't you wish you had a home? Someone to hold you? Someone to take care of you?"

The boy's innocent words lanced into Thorin. A

part of him—a part of him that he'd hidden deep inside him—wanted that.

He thought of Regan. The way she'd kissed him, touched him, the sweet taste of her. He released a harsh breath. Yes, he wanted someone to hold him. He wanted Regan to hold him.

He scrounged up some control and held onto his vow to protect her.

"I don't deserve a family," he said gruffly. "And I have a life here."

He felt the boy watching him.

Thankfully, they turned another corner and the metal fence of the spaceport lay straight ahead. Bright lights illuminated all the ships on the landing pads. Raiden waved them forward and they moved to an unguarded side gate, well out of security range.

Thorin set the boy down beside his brother.

"That's the ship over there." Raiden pointed to a bulky freighter. "The captain will be waiting for you."

"Here you go." Saff shoved a small bag at the oldest boy. "It has some clothes and other essentials."

"Thank you so much." The older brother gripped the bag tightly. "We can never repay what you've done for us."

"We don't want payment," Raiden said. "Now go."

"Be safe," Thorin told the younger boy.

"You, too." The boy leaned closer. "And everyone deserves someone to love them. No matter what."

With one final, long look, the boy turned and grabbed his brother's hand.

Thorin stood with the others, and they silently watched the boys cross the landing pads and reach the freighter. They waited until they saw their small forms enter the ship and disappear.

"It never gets old," Saff murmured.

No, helping people who didn't belong in the arena head home, was always satisfying. Thorin thought of Regan again. He wished he was able to send her back to where she belonged.

But she had no way home.

Their group melted back into the shadows, moving quickly back toward the arena.

"We'll take the southern entrance back in." Raiden moved up beside Thorin. "So, you seem rather overprotective of our new House of Galen member."

Thorin felt his neck stiffen. "Who?"

Raiden snorted. "Really? You're going to pretend you don't know who I'm talking about?"

"I'm just helping her out."

"Hmm. By tossing her over your shoulder and issuing her orders?"

Drak. Thorin stared into the darkness. He did *not* want to have this conversation.

"She's been through a lot, Thorin—"

"You have a point? If you're going to warn me to stay away from her, don't bother. There is no way I'd sully her with my hands."

"Hey." Raiden grabbed Thorin's arm and pulled him to a stop. "What the drak is that nonsense? I was going to warn you to tread carefully with her, but I've seen the way you watch her."

A muscle ticked in Thorin's jaw, but he stayed silent.

Raiden shook his head. "I've also seen the way she watches you."

Thorin shook his head. "You know better than anybody what I am. You know I can never have a small, soft female and not put her at risk."

"Thorin—"

"Just drop it, Raiden. I'm pleased you found Harper, but don't go trying to meddle with me."

Thorin charged ahead. Regan Forrest was not for him. No matter how much he might wish differently.

Chapter Six

Thorin watched Regan stride across the training arena. The morning sunlight was bright, both the suns moving into the sky. It reflected off the sand and made Regan's hair glint like gold.

Harper had obviously found her some training leathers, and they slicked over her slim legs and rounded curves.

He gritted his teeth. Any harder and he was pretty sure they were going to crack under the pressure.

"Any news on Rory?" she asked when she reached him.

"No."

Her face fell. "I know I need to be patient, but it's hard."

"Come on. We're going to try a few different weapons this morning." He led her over to the weapons rack. He eyed the weapons and realized they probably weighed almost as much as she did. He picked one of the smaller swords and held it out. She tried lifting it, but could barely get it off the ground.

He grabbed a large dagger. For him, it was

small, but for Regan, it was almost a short sword. "Try this for now."

He pulled a sword for himself and started showing her some basic moves. The axe was his weapon of choice. He liked the weight of it, but he kept up his training with the sword.

Step, step, thrust. Step, step, thrust. She followed his moves, watching him carefully. He knew that smart little mind of hers was working overtime. She did well and was damn near graceful when she moved.

He lost himself, watching her. She was right, she'd never be a gladiator. She didn't have the strength or the killer instinct for it. But he could teach her how to protect herself.

Thorin moved behind her to correct her stance, holding her elbow in close to her body. "Now move through that step again." Her rounded butt brushed against him. He hissed in a breath. *Drak.*

He stepped back and cleared his throat. "Try again."

She went through the moves again. When she moved wrong, he stepped in to correct her. Every time he got close, her curvy body brushed against his. It was driving him crazy.

"Again," he said hoarsely.

Her cheeks were pink now, a small smile flirting on her lips. "Okay, I've got it this time."

She moved the sword through the air, moving her feet through the sand. As she turned, her body brushed his again. Her face was flushed and covered in a sheen of sweat. She looked beautiful.

Thorin shifted, the pressure in his trousers beyond uncomfortable.

When she stepped back, her hip brushing against his, his gaze narrowed. She was brushing up against him on purpose.

He stepped away. "Good. Let's move on to another weapon," he told her. He grabbed up a net from the weapons rack. He held out the small, egg-shaped device.

She held it in her palm, testing its weight. "So this opens up into a net?"

He nodded. "All you need is pretty good aim, and the net will take your opponent down. It has sensors in it to help it target whatever's in its range."

She nodded and they moved over to some of the targets. There were several humanoid-shaped mannequins set up.

"Okay. Let's see how you do."

She pulled her arm back and tossed the net. It arrowed through the air and the net exploded outward. It slammed over the first mannequin.

"Yes!" She clapped her hands.

He smiled. She had good aim. It didn't take long for her to get the feel for the net. She was pretty damn good with it. He nodded. It was a good weapon for her, because it meant she didn't have to get too close to a bigger opponent.

"Good job," he told her.

She turned, shooting him a beaming smile. It was the happiest he'd seen her since they'd rescued her from the Thraxian ship. He knew she was still acclimating and was worried about her cousin. He felt a shot of warmth in his chest, somewhere in the vicinity of his heart.

Thorin cleared his throat. "I suggest you keep practicing with the net. It's a good weapon for you. When you take down your opponent, you turn and run. You don't have the strength or the training to tackle a larger fighter. So you get out of there."

She nodded. "Got it."

Thorin lifted his axe. "Okay, let's see how you do in a sparring match."

Her eyebrows lifted. "We're going to fight?"

He shifted his feet through the sand. "That's what we're here for."

She gave a determined nod, then lifted her sword and palmed a new net device. "Okay, big guy."

Soon they were circling each other. Thorin swung his axe at her a few times, watching as she ducked and weaved. She tossed the net device, but it sailed past him. The first few times, he laughed, and he could see she was getting angry, her brows drawn together.

"I think you need more practice, yet," he said with a grin.

As he turned around, the net struck him in the chest. The metallic ropes covered him, tangling him up and tripping him over.

She stood over him, her hands on her hips. "Who needs more practice now?"

He stared at her.

She bit down on her lip, looking like she was

trying to contain a laugh. She crouched, helping pull the net off him. "God, I'm sorry."

"No, you're not." He pulled the ropes away, glaring at her. "You're supposed to run."

She froze. "I'm not afraid of you. And I am sorry, you made me mad."

"You don't apologize to your opponent."

He sat up. Across the training arena, he could see Kace and Saff laughing their heads off.

Giggling, Regan grabbed the net and tossed it away. She was flushed and happy with herself. He rose, and a second later, she went up on her tiptoes and smacked a kiss against his jaw. It was quick, friendly.

But Thorin's hands came up and gripped her wrists. Her giggling died away.

"I said there was nothing between us. The kissing, the rubbing your sweet body against me...it has to stop."

They stared at each other, and he could feel it, the connection between them, filling the space, throbbing in the air. What the hell was it about this small woman that affected him like this?

"You want me," she said quietly. "I want you. I don't see what your problem is."

She was killing him and he needed some space between them. Thorin released her and waved Kace over. "Kace, take over Regan's training."

His friend nodded and Thorin shot Regan one last glance. She'd wrapped her arms around her middle, hurt stamped on her face. Steeling himself, he strode away, sand kicking up around his boots.

He needed to do something about this burning need, or he was going to lose his mind. He strode into the tunnels and then into their living quarters. A second later, he was in his room, slamming the door behind him. The wood rattled on its hinges.

He had to cool off. He needed some control. He, one of the best gladiators of the Kor Magna Arena, couldn't even control himself around one tiny woman.

He stormed into his bathroom. It had smooth, rock walls with a large bathing tub, and an even larger shower. He flicked on a control that had a waterfall of water streaming from the ceiling. He made sure the settings were turned to cold.

He stripped off his leathers and dumped them on the floor. Then he stepped under the cold stream.

It slicked over his body, but it didn't stop the images in his head. Of flushed cheeks and a pretty smile. Of a curvy female body brushing against him. Of the taste of her.

Thorin slid his hand down his abdomen, and circled his throbbing cock. He started to stroke himself. He needed some release. Maybe that would help him find the control he needed.

But as he roughly slid his hand up and down, it was still Regan in his head. He growled, pumping harder, desire twisting in his gut. It was her slim legs and wicked curves that had him spilling his seed all over the floor.

***

ANNA HACKETT

It was fight night again.

Regan sat in the stands, and this time, she didn't find the crowds so overwhelming. Maybe it was just that she knew what to expect now. But she knew that it wasn't just that. She knew that she was finding her footing, gaining her strength back. She'd kissed Thorin, teased him, yelled at him. They were all things the Regan she'd been before would have been terrified to do.

But the biggest feeling coursing through her veins tonight was excitement. She couldn't wait to watch Thorin fight, his big, powerful body moving across the sand. Harper was fighting tonight as well, and Regan was excited to see her friend in the arena.

"Would you like some *mahiz*?"

From beside her, Kace handed over a small bowl filled with a crunchy-looking snack. He was wearing a crisp blue shirt that matched his eyes, and dark trousers.

"What is it?" she asked.

"It's made from a vegetable. You cook it until it bursts open."

She placed some of the small, star-shaped pieces in her mouth. It was salty-tasting, and reminded her a little of popcorn.

"So Raiden's fighting with Harper tonight." She grabbed another handful of *mahiz*.

"Yes. And Saff is partnered with Thorin."

"You don't mind?"

He shook his head. "It is a pleasure to fight with Saff, but it's good to mix it up sometimes. You learn

68

more, and don't get complacent."

Regan nodded. She knew each of the gladiators had a partner. They practiced together, perfected their moves, and protected each other. Harper had told her it was unique to the House of Galen, and what gave them an edge.

Kace's face was so serious, and she wondered if he ever smiled. Whenever she was near Kace, she always felt like he was carrying a heavy weight. She knew he wasn't a slave, but was an arena volunteer, sent here by his military to hone his skills.

"Do you miss your planet?"

He glanced at her for a second. "I miss my work and my squad."

Suddenly, she felt the ground vibrating beneath her. A hush fell over the crowd. Regan shifted in her seat, dread curling in her belly. What was going on?

A moment later, the center of the arena floor opened up and six giant robots rose through the gap. Her eyes widened. She couldn't believe what she was seeing.

Fear trickled into her veins. The machines were enormous and humanoid in shape. "What the hell are those?"

"Tonight is a robot fight," Kace said, as the crowd started cheering, a wild sound reminiscent of thunder.

"Robot fight? The gladiators have to fight against those machines?" Her voice wavered.

"They'll be fine." Kace looked completely unconcerned.

The House of Galen gladiators entered the arena.

Harper and Raiden were in the lead, completely ignoring the crowd. Thorin and Saff came next, both of them raising their arms and egging the crowd on. Behind them, Nero and Lore brought up the rear.

As they closed in on the robots, even Thorin's powerful form looked small compared to the giant machines.

The first robot moved forward, swinging a huge club. Its blow smashed into the ground, sending up a cloud of dust. The crowd let out a fierce round of screams.

She saw the gladiators stop for a minute to talk. Then, with a wild roar, Thorin rushed forward. His big body powered forward as he ran. He swung his axe and attacked.

The robot's club swung down and Thorin dodged, rolling across the sand. He leaped back to his feet and ducked a swing of the robot's other arm. He slid in low, slamming his axe into one of the robot's legs.

The other gladiators fanned out, moving forward, but Regan only had eyes for Thorin.

The robot stamped its giant feet, sending more dust up, and narrowly missed Thorin. As the machine wielded its club again, Thorin threw his axe. It embedded itself in the robot's thigh, sending out a shower of sparks.

Thorin stood, and Saff came in from behind him. She threw her net, which tangled around the robot's legs. The machine started kicking, trying to get free. Thorin wrenched his axe out, pulled back, and slammed the weapon into the robot's knee, severing its leg.

The robot tilted over like a felled tree. It slammed into the ground, the lights blinking on its chest flickering before they went out.

The crowd surged to their feet, stamping and shouting.

Next, she watched Raiden and Harper sprinting together toward a second robot. They both ducked swings, their swords hacking into metal. Then Raiden lifted Harper, tossing her upward. Regan watched, heart in her throat, as her friend gripped the robot's arm and started climbing it. She nimbly scampered upward, keeping her balance as the machine moved. Then she grabbed the robot's shoulder and scrambled up. It shook itself, trying to get her loose, but she held on tight.

Harper climbed up behind the robot's head, and drew her swords. She reached forward and stabbed her blades into the robot's glowing eye sockets.

The machine went crazy. It started jerking and twisting. It swung around wildly, and Harper lost her balance. She flew backward through the air. The crowd gasped and Regan shot to her feet. *Harper.*

Raiden lifted his arms and snatched Harper out of the air. As the robot crumpled into a heap behind them, Raiden pulled Harper close and pressed a hard kiss to her lips.

They were so alive. So in love. Regan pressed her palm to her racing heart. The arena was violent, physical, but there was just something about it. It stripped everything back to raw emotion. Watching these gladiators testing themselves to their limits, working together as a team, wrung out all kinds of emotions from the crowd.

Lore took down another robot, and then spun to face the crowd. He clapped his hands and smoke rose up above the arena floor, like a storm cloud.

The smoke changed colors, turning to the red-and-gray colors of the House of Galen. Lore spun elegantly, and red confetti rained down like rose petals.

The crowd loved it. It also provided cover for Nero as he charged in against another robot with whirling blades at the end of its arms. He fought with relentless determination and power, and soon the robot was nothing more than twisted metal on the sand.

That left two more robots.

Regan watched, her heart hammering against her ribs, as Thorin and Saff brought the next one down. As it slammed onto its back on the ground, Thorin leaped up on its chest and brought his axe down. He was like a wild man, ripping and tearing until he pulled out the robot's mechanical heart.

He held it up above his head, and the crowd screamed his name. Regan screamed it loudest of all.

***

Thorin's chest was heaving. He shifted and he realized that his scales were out. Bloodlust was riding him.

A good fight always did that. He looked up, his gaze unconsciously searching the crowd, and he spotted Regan. She was cheering, her arms lifted above her head. Cheering for him.

Lust slammed into him. Drak, he wanted her to watch him. To see his strength and skills. To see *him*.

Even across the distance, he saw her go still, their gazes locked. He knew she could feel it. He knew that she was thinking of him touching her, sucking her, him moving thickly inside her body.

The sound of fighting made him rip his gaze away. The others had brought the final robot to its knees, but its weapon was a dangerous electrical charge that sizzled across its body.

Feeling pumped, Thorin charged forward. With a mighty roar, he swung his axe and slammed it into the robot's chest. Sparks flew in a wild shower around him.

As he yanked his axe out of the metal and stepped back, the rest of his team rushed forward to finish off the giant machine.

He glanced at Regan again, and she was still cheering.

He stood there, feeling that last rush of energy through his body. He was soaked in sweat, and while there was no blood tonight, he was surrounded by torn metal and ruined components. Destruction.

No. He was supposed to be staying away from Regan. She deserved better than this, and this wasn't even the worst of what he was capable of. He needed to get this *thing* under control.

Sweating and beating things in training and in the arena wasn't working. Jerking off in his hand wasn't working, either. He needed to try something else.

As he turned, the announcers declared the House of Galen the victors.

Raiden stepped up beside him and slapped him on the back. "You were on fire tonight, my friend."

"We owned the sand," Saff called out.

As a group, they turned and headed toward the tunnels. Thorin lifted a hand to the cheering crowd, but paid them little attention. Emotions were twisting inside him. He felt something stir deep in his chest. *Drak.*

In the tunnel, he saw Regan waiting for them. She was so pretty, so clean.

She was the light. And he was dark. He'd been born dark, honed in blood-drenched shadows, and nothing would ever change that.

She smiled at him and a lick of panic went through him. He had to do something, or he was going to succumb, claim her as his, and never let her go. She had no comprehension of what that truly meant.

She started walking toward him, and he knew

that this time he couldn't turn her away.

Suddenly, two women rushed in front of her in a cloud of perfume. The two flutterers rushed up to him, screaming his name.

Both women were tall, toned, with long waves of black hair and beautiful faces. One latched onto his side, while the other pressed herself against his chest, her hands sliding under his leather harness.

He looked down at them and felt...nothing. Desire was throbbing through him, but it was for one woman only. The one woman he'd vowed to stay away from.

"Kiss me, Thorin!" One of the women pressed a kiss to his jaw. "I want it hard and dirty, gladiator."

He looked up, and saw Regan watching him, frozen.

He felt Raiden and Harper go still beside him.

Then Thorin nodded. "Sure thing, gorgeous."

Instantly, she smacked her mouth against his, her tongue thrusting inside his mouth. He held himself still for a few seconds, but then he couldn't stomach it. He lifted his head and looked up just in time to see Regan's stricken face.

The second woman at his side splayed her hand across his abs, sliding downward. He grabbed her fingers before she slid them inside the front of his leathers.

This time when he looked up, Regan was gone.

Raiden stepped past him, shaking his head. "Idiot."

Chapter Seven

Regan worked all through the night. She knew she was moving maniacally, rushing from test to test, and experiment to experiment. But she wanted to get the med gel ready, and she needed to keep busy.

She needed to keep her mind off Thorin.

Just his name made her muscles lock. Images blasted through her head of him lying back in his big bed, naked women crawling all over him.

She dropped a glass beaker and it smashed on the stone floor. *Dammit.*

Regan forced herself to take a few calming breaths. Then she bent down to clean up the mess. A piece of glass pricked her finger and she snatched her hand back. A tiny bead of blood bloomed, and she stuck her finger in her mouth. It was nothing. Nothing compared to the hurt in her chest.

She sighed. Thorin wasn't hers, had never been hers. She looked up, her gaze running across the crowded benches of her lab. This was her space. This was where she belonged. Tears pricked her eyes and she fought them back. She had no business chasing after a big, wild gladiator.

She was Dr. Regan Forrest. Nice, sensible scientist. She'd fought against her parents' expectations to forge her career. They'd wanted her to be something else, and it appeared Thorin wanted something else, too.

No one ever accepted Regan for herself.

Stop feeling sorry for yourself, Regan. She stood and straightened her simple blue top. She just had to focus on what she had achieved. The enhanced med gel was ready. She carried out all the tests she'd wanted and she knew it was much better than the original product. She also had tests running on various different liniments to help loosen up sore muscles. She turned her head to the ledge by the window holding all her plants. And she'd managed to get a dead stalk to bloom into a beautiful flower. It was the most luscious red, edged in white. The bloom had three petals, each a curl with a fluted edge. And the scent—she breathed deep—she'd never smelled anything quite as beautiful.

Yes, she'd focus on her work and not the stubborn gladiator who'd cracked her heart.

She pressed her palms to the surface of the bench. *Damn him.* There was no need for him to knife her like that and rub it in her face. Regan tucked a strand of hair back behind her ears.

At some point during the long, lonely night, she'd realized that she was dependent on everyone here in the House of Galen. She'd been using Thorin for comfort and protection, Harper for emotional support, and Galen for everything else.

She had no money, and was dependent on what others gave her.

If this was going to be her home, she needed to find a way to support herself. It was time for her to stand up for herself.

She grabbed a small knife and the finished tube of med gel off the bench. Then she tossed a small cloth over the blooming plant and carried it under one arm. It was delicate and didn't like too much light.

She knew it was still early, but she marched out of her lab and down the corridor toward Galen's office. The large wooden door was inlaid with a metal version of the house logo—that fierce profile of a gladiator.

She didn't knock, just slammed inside.

Galen's head shot up. He was sitting behind a giant, wooden desk. Behind him, the large, arched windows offered a beautiful view of the rising suns and the empty training arena below.

He scowled at her, and with his eye patch across his scarred face, she thought he looked like some angry warrior of the gods.

"And good morning to you," he said in his deep voice. "Just come in."

She blew out a breath. "Sorry." She didn't need to take her anger out on other people. "Do you have a few minutes?"

He leaned back in his chair, and waved a hand at one of the chairs in front of his desk. Up close, she saw the desk was made from a dark, grained wood. His large desk chair was made from the leather of some animal.

She sank into the guest chair and set her things down on the desk. "First of all, I want to thank you for taking me in. I've been busy settling in, and wrapping my head around everything—"

He frowned. "Wrapping your head—?"

"Sorry. An Earth saying. Trying to understand everything. I haven't really said thank you. I know I'm not a gladiator, but I want to find a way to earn my keep. To make my own living."

Galen studied her, that single, pale-blue eye like a laser. Regan got the impression the man was good at reading people very quickly.

He rested his hands on the desk. "I'm listening."

She moved the med gel tube to the center of his desk.

One of his eyebrows rose.

Maybe it was better if she just showed him. She pulled out the knife and cut it across her palm, wincing at the pain.

Galen pushed his chair back and jumped to his feet. "Hell."

"It's okay." She reached out and squeezed some of the gel on her palm. "I've been working on enhancing the med gel properties." She held her palm out so he could see as the edges of the wound sealed together. "A wound that used to take hours to heal will now heal in just minutes."

He sank slowly into his chair, a gleam in his eye. "Well done."

"Thanks. I'm a botanist with a specialty in healing properties of plants. That's what I did before. I've collected all the plants I could find around here and have been studying them." She felt a wash of heat in her cheeks. "It's my thing."

"It's impressive."

She shrugged. "Not quite as impressive as fighting giant gladiators in the arena."

He watched her intently. "I disagree. It's just different."

His praise made her chest warm.

"What else have you been working on?" he asked.

"I'm working on a few other things right now, but nothing's quite ready yet." She shrugged her shoulder. "My only other small success is something I don't think you'll care about."

"Try me."

She lifted the cloth off the flower. Its beautiful scent wafted around them.

A funny look crossed Galen's face. "Do you know what that is?"

She frowned. "A flower. Well, it was a dead stalk in the living area, before." She shifted nervously. "I didn't think anyone would mind if I took it. I just watered and fertilized it."

"It's called an *oria*."

"Okay." It sounded pretty.

"Regan, it's the rarest flower in the galaxy. Said to be created by the Creators themselves."

Regan tilted her head, curiosity rising. "The alien species who seeded life throughout the galaxy?" She still couldn't wrap her head around the idea that an advanced species traveled the galaxy millions of years ago, planting life on various planets, like cosmic gardeners.

"Yes. The *oria* is highly prized for its scent, and even worshipped by some species. This one was a gift from a very pleased and very wealthy sponsor. We tried desperately to keep it alive, without success—as you know. It's worth as much as I pay my gladiators each year."

Her mouth dropped open. She reached out to finger the bloom. "Oh."

Galen leaned forward. "What I pay *all* of my gladiators added together."

She snatched her hand back. "Oh, my God."

He shot her a faint smile. "I think I can find a buyer for you. For the gel and the *oria*."

"Buyer? Oh, well, they're not really mine. I was just hoping that you'd pay me a wage to work on this stuff—"

"You create it, it's yours. The House of Galen will take a cut, but the rest belongs to you."

She dropped into the chair. "Wow."

He smiled again, and it did nothing to soften his intimidating face. "Good work. I'll set up a meeting for the sale in the market. I'll ask Thorin to accompany you."

"No." The word burst out of her.

Galen's eye narrowed.

She swallowed. "I mean, yes, please, to the meeting. But not Thorin. Maybe someone else?"

Galen kept watching her.

"Please," she whispered.

Finally, he nodded. "In the meantime, continue

your work in your lab."

Despite the hurt still lodged in her chest, Regan felt something inside her ease. She wasn't dependent on anyone, anymore.

Maybe she could actually make a life here, all by herself.

***

Thorin lifted his bottle of ale and took a sip. He was sprawled in a chair in the living area, not interested in talking to anybody. He watched the morning light slowly moving across the floor.

Slowly, the others started to file in.

Lore raised a hand, his long hair still tangled. "You look like you didn't get much sleep."

Thorin lifted his bottle again, wordlessly. It was the truth.

A door opened and Harper strode in. She shot him a scathing look before she headed over to the area where the kitchen workers had laid out breakfast.

Nero lumbered in. "Heard there's a sandstorm brewing to the west. Should be fun."

The electrical sandstorms on Carthago could be spectacular...and dangerous. Everyone would have to hunker inside and wait it out. If they were lucky, the storm would shift direction and not hit Kor Magna. If they weren't, well, the storm would match Thorin's mood.

Raiden's heavy footsteps sounded and his friend paused beside Thorin's chair. "Ale for breakfast?"

Thorin grunted. "Finishing my night of celebration."

"Right. I heard you send those women on their way."

Thorin tensed, his fingers curling on the bottle.

Raiden sat in a chair next to him and stretched out his legs. He pitched his voice lower, after casting a quick glance around the room. "And you sent them off right after we got back here. So either your staying power has dropped significantly, or you didn't take them up on their offers."

Thorin took another deliberate sip of ale. "You have a point?"

"I take it the show was for Regan. What I don't get is why?"

Thorin stayed silent.

"She likes you, Thorin. You don't want her, then just tell her. Some other lucky bastard will snap her up."

The bottle in Thorin's hand shattered, glass splintering all over the floor. The room instantly quieted. He dropped his voice even lower. "I want her more than I draking want to breathe, Raiden."

His friend frowned. "So what's stopping you—?"

"I'm no good for her."

"Bullshit."

Thorin turned his head, frowning at the foreign word. "What does that mean?"

"It's an Earth word I learned from Harper. It means you're lying and full of crap. You deserve a woman full of goodness. A woman like Regan." Raiden's gaze moved over to Harper. "They change you, even things out, make everything better and more worthwhile." Raiden's green gaze met Thorin's. "It feels good."

"You know where I came from. You saw me at my worst when I got here." Hell, without Raiden, Thorin would have self-destructed long ago. "You know what I am."

"Still bullshit." Raiden leaned forward. "You aren't one tiny bit of your heritage, Thorin. You are the man you've made yourself. You are a good friend, a good gladiator, and a good man."

Drak. Thorin stared at his hands. He wanted to believe that, but he refused to do anything that could jeopardize Regan.

Another door opened, and Galen walked in. "Listen up. One of my informants got back to me. I might have some clues to Rory's location."

The atmosphere in the room changed, turned more focused. They all moved over to the table, where Galen laid out a sheet of paper.

"First, I need to know if this is her."

Harper shouldered closer. Thorin looked at the image and saw a woman with an interesting face, a pointed chin, and a tough look in her gold-flecked green eyes. Deep-red curls—a unique shade he'd never seen before—twisted around her face.

Harper let out a shaky breath. "That's her. That's Rory." Harper smiled briefly. "She's still here and she's alive. So what's next?"

"Regan's information was correct. The Thraxians had her, but then sold her in a private sale." Galen said.

"What does that mean?" Harper asked with a frown.

"It means if we find out who attended the private sale, we can narrow down who has her."

"How do we find out who was at the sale?" Lore asked.

"I'm working on that," Galen said, tapping a finger against the table. "Another contact said he can get me the guest list for the sale. Unfortunately, he works on his own schedule and only at night."

"Zhim," Thorin said. The merchant sold information, was the best on Carthago and cost a pretty credit as well.

Galen's mouth flattened. "Unfortunately, yes."

Thorin stood. "Regan will want to know this." He took two steps, heading toward her room.

"She's not here," Galen said, stopping him.

Thorin fought a clutch in his stomach. "Where is she?"

"She's gone to the market."

Thorin stiffened. "Alone?"

"No. I sent her with Kace." Galen stared at him. "Strangely, she didn't want you to go with her."

Thorin absorbed the blow. Clean-cut, handsome Kace was just the kind of man that Regan deserved. The man was contained, controlled and never lost his cool, even in the middle of a fight. He didn't party with women, he didn't overindulge, and he was a hell of a fighter. He'd protect her.

A muscle ticked in Thorin's jaw. *Drak*. He turned and stormed out.

***

Regan handed over the tube of med gel and took the coins in return. She smiled at the alien woman and thanked her.

She knew there was an electronic credit system in use on Carthago, mainly in the District, but here in the market, Galen had warned her the locals preferred to barter, trade coins, or run tabs with use of a token for those they trusted.

Regan turned to move back into the market. She stared down at the gold coins glinting in her hands and grinned.

"Better tuck those away."

She smiled up at Kace and shoved the coins in her pocket. "Thanks for coming with me."

A faint smile appeared on the gladiator's lips. "It's my pleasure."

His face was sharp planes and a strong jaw, and there was no denying he was handsome. He wouldn't have looked out of place as an action hero in a blockbuster movie back on Earth. But she'd seen him fight, with a military precision and focus that was more than a little scary.

She studied Kace in more detail. Sleek muscles, bronze skin, and that face. She couldn't see the torment and darkness that she saw in Thorin. Kace had this containment and control about him, but... She tilted her head, studying his blue eyes. There was something lurking there.

"We better get back to the House of Galen." Kace

pointed her in the right direction.

All around them, the hustle and bustle of the market was a loud din. Being underground, the noise of conversations and the shouts of hawkers echoed off the stone walls. Nearby, she could smell something cooking.

"I'm glad we got rid of the *oria* first," Regan said. She'd been nervous as hell, carrying around the plant shrouded in a cloth and knowing how much it was worth.

Kace's small smile widened. "Me too. They are revered on my planet."

"Really?"

He nodded. "If you look closely at my arm guard at the next fight, you'll see a stylized *oria* engraved on it. I'd never seen one up close before."

She snorted. "You've been eating your meals around it every day in the living area."

"I just thought it was a stick."

Galen had been true to his word. He'd organized a buyer for the *oria*. The small man they'd met had almost fallen over himself to take the plant. He'd transferred credits to an account Galen had organized for her. She couldn't imagine carrying so many coins around.

And now she'd sold her med gel, and had organized a standing arrangement to sell more tubes to the woman who ran a healing center here in Kor Magna every month.

They'd stepped under one of the sinkholes. It was much smaller than the one used as an entrance. This one acted like a skylight to the subterranean market.

Regan looked up, the sunlight bathing her face. She could see an ornate grate covering the hole, to stop a wayward person falling into it. Despite the aches she still carried inside, thanks to a certain gladiator, she was feeling okay.

"You're a wealthy woman now." Kace moved closer, maneuvering her through the crowd.

She managed a smile. "Maybe I'll head to the District and try some gambling. I hear the casinos are incredible." She shook her head. "I was completely broke when I woke up this morning."

"It doesn't actually look like you woke up this morning."

She frowned up at him. "What do you mean?"

He reached out and gently touched under one of her eyes. "You don't look like you slept at all."

She hunched her shoulders. "I was busy in my lab."

"Right. Thorin's an idiot."

"I don't want to talk about him." She pushed forward, quickening her stride. As they moved along the stalls and tunnels spearing off into different parts of the market, she watched Kace scanning the crowd ahead. He used his big body to keep people from bumping into her. It seemed all these House of Galen gladiators had the protector gene.

"I see the way you look at him," Kace said.

She stayed silent, her fingers curling into her palms.

"And the way he looks at you."

She stopped, her hands clenching in the folds of her dress. "He took some of those women, the gladiator fans, back to his room last night. He made his choice."

Kace made an unconvinced sound. He turned her down a tunnel. "This is a shortcut back to the entrance. Look, Thorin's...complicated."

"It's really not that complicated, Kace. Wanting someone, wanting to be with them, shouldn't be complicated. Not if you want someone just the way they are." Her heart felt like it was squeezing into a tiny ball. "I'm not asking Thorin to change who he is. I know all about that. I've had everyone in my life wanting me to do something else or be something else just to please them." She wouldn't do the same to Thorin.

Suddenly, Kace went still, his gaze focused ahead of them. He reached out and pulled her closer.

She looked ahead. The tunnel was completely empty and wreathed in shadows.

A feeling of wrongness fell over her, and her muscles tensed, one by one. The tunnel should be busy; the lights should be on.

Suddenly, a man rushed out of the darkness.

Kace thrust Regan back, and she stumbled. Two more men lunged forward, joining the first. The men all charged at Kace. The gladiator fought with his usual lethal intensity. The sounds of kicks, hits, and hard punches echoed off the walls. Kace managed to take several men down, before a tall woman stepped into the light and jabbed some sort of device into Kace's side. The next second, Regan watched as blue electricity ran all over Kace's body.

He froze in place, his body shuddering and his back arching. He managed to turn his head and look at her. She saw his lips move.

Run.

Regan spun and sprinted.

She heard them coming after her. Heard their pounding footsteps. The end of the tunnel looked light years away.

Arms wrapped and lifted her off her feet.

Fear arrowed through her. It felt like she was back with the Thraxians. She struggled and kicked, and then the electrical shock hit her.

She dropped to her knees, all her muscles twitching and no longer under her control. It hurt. It hurt so bad.

She struggled to breathe, to see, not to panic. Then she passed out.

Chapter Eight

Thorin pushed through the crowd, trying to spot Kace or Regan.

Some stall owners he'd questioned had told him they'd taken the eastern tunnel out of the market.

They'd also gushed about the tiny woman from Earth who'd been charming, happy, and excited. Thorin hated that he'd missed being there to see her sell her things.

He stepped into the eastern tunnel, and spotted a concerned crowd milling and talking.

He pushed forward. "What's going on?"

As the crowd parted, he saw Kace lying facedown on the ground. Beaten, bloodied, and unconscious. A few people were trying to help him, and someone would have recognized Kace and sent word to Galen.

Drak. Thorin dropped to his knees. "Kace?" He checked the gladiator's life signs, then slapped his cheek. "Come on, Kace. Time to wake up."

The man slowly started to move. Thorin lifted his head, hoping to spot Regan in the crowd. She wasn't there. Panic made his throat close. Where was she?

"Kace," he said more urgently.

ANNA HACKETT

The man's eyes opened. They looked clouded and unfocused. "I'm okay."

Thorin helped him sit up. "Take it easy."

"They stunned me." As Kace leaned forward, he groaned. "It hurts like the fires of Vulca."

Thorin grabbed the man's shoulders. "Where's Regan?"

Kace stiffened, his eyes clearing. "After they jumped me, I told her to run. Did she get back to the House of Galen?"

Damn. Thorin had a bad feeling about this.

"You're looking for the woman?" An older man moved forward. "The small woman?"

Thorin pushed to his feet. "Yes. You saw her?"

"They took her. She fought hard."

No. Thorin speared the man with a hard look. "Get a message to the House of Galen. Inform them that Regan has been taken. Go."

The man swallowed and, with a nod, ran off.

"No one move," Thorin demanded. "I need to take a look at the signs on the ground."

He moved in methodical circles, staring at the hard-packed, sandy ground. He could pick out where the crowd moved in and out of the tunnel to help Kace. But then he also noted the signs of a struggle in the sand.

Kace had put up a hell of a fight.

Then he spotted Regan's smaller footprints. Thorin crouched, touching them gently. They were surrounded by far larger ones. He followed her prints until they abruptly disappeared. He saw the place where she'd fallen, and then someone had picked her up.

Had they hurt her? Was she dead?

He shut down his thoughts straight away, and pulled in a deep breath. All he could focus on was finding her. He picked up the faint smell of her scent.

"Can you track her?" Kace was beside him, swaying a little.

"I've got her scent. We'll see how far I can track her." Thorin vowed he would go to the ends of the planet, if that's what it took.

Kace took a step to follow him.

Thorin rounded on him. "You're in no condition—"

"I'm coming," Kace said, tone unyielding.

Finally, Thorin gave him a nod. They moved together, going through the back tunnels, the ones less used, less populated. This was the dark underbelly of the market, the place where you could find the things that weren't so pretty or legal. He followed the elusive smell, that sweet, sweet scent of Regan. Every now and then, he spotted some of the larger footprints he'd seen back at the fight zone.

Then he saw Regan's footsteps again. She'd gotten loose and run, but they'd tackled her. There was a patch of ground with larger markings and a tiny handprint. She'd obviously been knocked down and they'd kicked her. He saw a drop of ruby-red blood staining the sand.

Regan's blood.

As his hand curled into a giant fist, his knuckles

ANNA HACKETT

cracked. Someone would pay.

Finally, they reached the end of the tunnel. It split in two directions. One headed downward to the levels where he knew some of Kor Magna's poorer residents lived—those who couldn't afford houses on the surface.

The other direction lead to a very large sinkhole shaft that was outfitted with a transport lift to move goods to and from the surface. The faintest trace of her scent led down that tunnel. His gut cramped. Damn, if they got her to the surface and into a transport before he could catch them, he'd lose her. He wouldn't be able to follow her trail.

He turned toward the lift and moved faster, Kace at his heels.

They charged out of the tunnel.

"Drak," Kace cursed.

Thorin's head jerked up. A bulky transport with its back doors open sat on the lift platform. A group of people was trying to force Regan inside the back of the vehicle.

She was struggling, fighting like a wild woman.

In the back of the transport, Thorin spotted a cage.

He reached over his shoulder and yanked out his axe. They were trying to force her into a cage. Something dark and dangerous stirred inside him. A part of him he hadn't felt in a long time.

He didn't make a sound as he charged toward them. A red haze covered his vision. Before they even knew he was there, he swung his axe and took down two of her attackers.

As he swung at the next man, he glimpsed Regan's pale, terrified face.

Thorin kept swinging, taking down another attacker, then another. He saw a man and a woman back away from him.

"Not getting paid enough for this," the woman muttered. They turned and ran.

But Thorin lunged forward, and caught the man by the back of his shirt. He'd been the one with his hands on Regan, trying to shove her into the cage.

Thorin swung the man around and then slammed him facefirst into the mesh side of the lift. He turned his head and watched as Kace threw a knife. It flew through the air and hit the escaping female attacker in the back. She stumbled forward, hitting the ground.

With methodical precision fueled by the dark part of him he kept hidden, Thorin swung his prey around. Thorin realized his arms were covered in scales, but he didn't care. He started hammering the man with punches. Soon, the man sagged, his screams turning to pained moans.

"Thorin!"

An annoying voice he ignored.

"Thorin, enough." Kace shouldered in front of him. "Regan needs you."

That made Thorin pause and drop the man. "Regan." He turned and saw her standing there, shivering.

He opened his arms and she leaped at him, her small body slamming against his chest. "They were going to take me."

He wrapped his arms around her, the dark scales on his arms looking wrong against her pale skin. But she hadn't hesitated to come to him. She needed him. "You're safe."

"Thorin." A shudder ran through her. "Get me away from the cage."

As she burrowed against his chest, warmth exploded inside him. He held her, turning away from the transport.

"You're safe now. You're safe." He could feel the frantic flutter of her pulse under her skin.

"You came for me," she whispered, pressing her cheek to his bare chest.

"Always." She was safe, and he was going to keep her that way. He swung her into his arms.

"They're getting away," Kace said quietly.

Thorin saw the few attackers who could still stand dragging their friends into the lift. He fought the violent urge to go after them and demand to know who the hell hired them, and why they wanted Regan.

But as she curled into him, still shaking, he held onto her. Regan was his priority. The lift clanged as it started upward.

"Let's get her home." He nodded at Kace for them to leave.

***

It wasn't until they got back to the House of Galen, that Regan finally drew a big breath and felt her muscles unlock. She held onto Thorin and the warm, solid comfort he gave her.

Once they were inside, though, memories of the night before crashed into her. Other women had been pressed up against his chest just hours before. Her stomach curdled.

She pushed against him. She felt his arms tighten for a second and he then reluctantly let her down.

She refused to look at him. "Thank you for rescuing me."

"Regan!" The sound of running footsteps.

Harper ran toward her and threw her arms around Regan. "We heard what happened. Are you all right?"

She gripped her friend. "Yes. Thorin and Kace rescued me." Regan lifted her head. "Kace? They hurt you. Are you okay?"

The gladiator nodded, blood staining his face. Even though his face looked impassive, his hands were curled into tight fists by his sides and anger radiated off him. "I'm fine, Regan. I'm sorry they took you."

"Don't be sorry. You fought like a machine and there were so many of them."

She turned stiffly to Thorin. "Thanks again for coming after me."

"I'll always come after you."

Right. Unless he was busy cavorting with beautiful, sexy women who threw themselves at him. She stomped on the nasty thought. She had to move past these feelings.

"Come on." Harper slid her arm around Regan's

shoulders. "You need a drink and some rest."

Regan let her friend take charge, and she didn't look at Thorin as they left. Soon she found herself being urged to sit down in a comfy chair in the living area, and a glass of water was pushed into her hand.

Raiden moved closer and touched a spot on her face. "You have a graze. You need some of your new med gel."

"Kace needs it more than me."

"I'll get it," Harper said.

Raiden stared at Regan for a second, then crouched down. "He didn't sleep with them."

"Kace?" She frowned, not quite sure what he was talking about.

"Thorin. He sent those women away once you were out of sight."

A part of Regan screamed in joy, but she pulled her sensible scientist side around her and shut it down. "It doesn't matter. He doesn't want me, Raiden, and I got the message. Loud and clear." Her voice dropped to a whisper. "He should have just told me he didn't want me. I'm used to people not wanting me."

Raiden sighed. "He doesn't believe he's worthy of you. Of love. Of more." The tattooed gladiator shoved a hand through his hair. "If you knew about his past, how he came to be here—"

"His brother sold him."

Raiden's eyes widened. "He told you?"

She gave her a small nod. "That's all he said."

"There's more to the story, but he's never told

anyone that much but me."

Regan's heart clenched.

Harper reappeared. "Enough. She needs to rest. Let's get you cleaned up, Regan."

***

Thorin slammed into Galen's office.

The imperator raised a brow and stood from his desk chair. He set a glowing screen down beside a stack of papers. "No, you aren't disturbing me. Come right on in."

"Someone tried to snatch Regan." Fury ran through Thorin's veins like acid. "I want to know who it was." He wanted the crud-spawn's head under his axe.

"I know. I already have Lore and Nero looking into it."

Thorin slammed a fist against the wall. "They took down Kace, grabbed her, frightened her." He remembered the way she clung to him. "They were trying to force her into a cage, G."

Galen skirted the desk, then leaned back against it. His icy gaze was on Thorin. "She's safe. You brought her back and she's unharmed."

"Who the hell has the balls to try and take someone who has House of Galen protection?"

"We'll find out." Galen's words held a dark promise.

Thorin sensed someone in the doorway and spotted a grim-faced Kace. His face was still covered in blood.

"It was my fault," Kace said. "They ambushed us and—"

Galen made a sound. "The intel I've gathered said you were outnumbered and fought multiple attackers. And you managed to injure quite a few of them. This isn't your fault, Kace."

The clean-cut gladiator stood straight and still. His expression didn't change.

Galen sighed. "Get down to Medical and get that wound healed."

Kace gave a single nod, then glanced at Thorin. "I'm sorry, Thorin." He turned and left.

"And you—" Galen speared Thorin with a look "—give me some time and we *will* work out who was behind this. I do know that the team who attacked Regan was a mercenary-for-hire squad. They work for the highest bidder."

"It has to be the Thraxians." Just the thought of those bastards getting their hands on Regan again was enough to make Thorin's fingers itch to grab his axe.

"We don't know that yet. Give it time."

Now Thorin understood why Regan risked leaving the House of Galen to follow the House of Thrax workers. Waiting for information was worse than landing facefirst in arena sand.

A knock sounded at Galen's door. One of the security guards, dressed in gray and red, stood at the doorway.

"I'm sorry, Imperator Galen," the woman said. "I just needed to inform you that the sandstorm we were monitoring has changed course and is heading for Kor Magna."

Galen sighed. "Just what we needed. Fine, give the orders for the staff to install the storm shutters. Lock down the training arena and ensure all workers are home well before the storm hits."

"Yes, Imperator."

After the guard left, Galen moved, gripping Thorin's arm. "I swear to you, we'll find out who tried to take her."

The imperator had never lied to Thorin, and Galen was a man who always delivered on his promises.

Thorin gave a nod.

"In the meantime, you don't let Regan out of your sight. You keep her safe."

Thorin straightened. That meant staying close to her, no space between them. Every minute of every day exposed to her sweet body. He released a breath.

"That's right," Galen said. "Whatever demons you're battling in regard to that woman, you need to set them aside. For her sake."

But what if the demon was you, and the battle was one he wasn't sure he could beat?

It didn't matter. What mattered was Regan, and Thorin would do whatever he had to do to keep Regan safe.

Chapter Nine

Regan rolled over in her bed, shifting to try and untangle the sheets from her legs.

She sighed and flopped back against the pillows. Her nightmares weren't letting her sleep. The roar of the wind outside wasn't helping.

A flash of lightning flickered through the shutters, and then a deafening crack of thunder shook the entire compound.

Wrapping her arms around herself, she slid out of the bed. A few hours ago, a siren had blasted across the city, warning the citizens that a massive dust storm was incoming. The House of Galen workers had leaped into action, installing large wooden shutters over all the windows. She peeked through the tiny gap in the slats. Sand whirled around outside.

Apparently, deadly electrical sandstorms were common here on Carthago. She watched as a giant spear of lightning branched through the sky. The hair on her arms rose, the energy in the air rushing across her skin.

She'd always loved thunderstorms back on Earth. She'd wanted to run around in the rain and watch the lightning, while her horrified parents had looked at her like they'd wondered where she'd come from.

But she wasn't on Earth anymore. She couldn't get a good view of the storm from here, and decided she was going to find a better vantage point. She quietly crept out of her room, and padded through the living area. She headed down the corridor, her bare feet silent on the stone, and over to the little balcony she'd claimed as her own. Shutters had been installed here as well, but the gaps between the slats were wider, and as she stepped out the door, the wind tore at her white nightgown, sending it billowing. Her hair whipped around her shoulders.

She touched the shutters, opening one a little wider. She watched the violent sandstorm and the lightning sparking through it. She felt alive, electric.

And tonight, she was grateful not to be back in a cage. She wrapped her arms around herself and shivered.

"You shouldn't be here."

Thorin's deep voice had her turning. He stood there, framed by the doorway, his arms crossed over his very broad and very naked chest.

She felt like the lightning was running through her, now. His chest was almost always naked, but every time she saw it, it still took her breath away.

There was another crack of thunder. Regan felt as though the two of them were in their own cocoon, surrounded by the storm. He stood there, so big, so alpha, so strong. She let her gaze skate over his huge arms, his strong jaw, and his bare chest. He was only wearing a pair of loose-fitting gray trousers that draped over his strong legs and the large bulge of his cock.

Regan let out a shuddering breath. She wanted this man so much, even though he confused her. He pushed her away with one hand and held her close with the other. She wanted to touch him, to press her hands over all those muscles, and circle that enormous cock.

Heat raced over her skin, flushing her cheeks. She was so turned on she hurt. Another crash of thunder rumbled.

She could see that his harsh breathing was making his chest heave. His hands were fists at his sides, and she could clearly see the strained muscles in his neck.

She desperately wanted to touch him.

"Go back to bed, Regan." He turned and strode away.

She closed her eyes. The wind was rushing through the shutters, and now she felt hot and cold as the wind tore at her. The urge to go after him was so strong, matching the pulse between her legs and the need clawing at her.

But she wouldn't. This time, he had to come to her.

Quickly, Regan secured the shutters and raced back to her room. As lightning hit again, she rushed into her room, throwing the door closed behind her.

Her skin felt too sensitive, her breasts swollen,

her senses heightened to almost intolerable levels. She dropped back onto her bed, pulling at her nightgown. She'd never thought of herself as a sexual creature. Sex could be nice and fun, but she'd never felt this way before. Like she was burning up. She wanted to blame the storm, but she knew there was only one man to blame. One man who made her feel like a burning inferno.

She imagined Thorin's big body on hers, his rough hands spreading her thighs, his mouth dragging across her breasts.

She was never going to get any sleep. She lay back and shoved the fabric of her nightgown up to her waist. Then she let her hand drift down, over her soft belly, before it slipped between her thighs. She touched herself, swallowing a little moan. She was already damp and she imagined Thorin's hand on her, his mouth and the scruff on his jaw scraping against her most sensitive parts.

Anticipation made her shake. Finally, she touched her clit, making a little mewling sound. She rubbed it, her legs shifting on the bed.

She was so empty. She reached down and slid her finger inside herself, but it wasn't enough. It wasn't Thorin.

Then she heard a pained sound. A cross between a groan and growl. She jerked, her eyes flying open.

Thorin stood in the doorway.

His face was twisted, color riding high on his cheekbones. Those elusive dark scales were visible on his arms and chest.

Their gazes locked, both of them breathing fast.

Apart from the thunder and howl of the wind, only Thorin's harsh breathing filled the space.

Regan's belly contracted. She kept touching herself and she saw his gaze go there. With him watching her, she felt naughty, sexy.

"Don't stop." His voice was a deep growl. "Keep touching yourself."

She licked her lips. This couldn't be her. She was a sensible scientist. Dr. Regan Forrest didn't lie sprawled on a bed, touching herself in front of a man.

No, not just a man. A big, sexy alien gladiator.

But she spread her legs wider, her thumb circling her clit. Her gaze never left him.

There was more lightning again, illuminating his large form in harsh white light. He should be frightening, but looking at him just increased her desire.

She moved her fingers faster, and as she watched him, she saw one of his big hands slide down his ridged abs. He cupped the giant bulge in his pants and her eyes widened. It was enormous now, straining the fabric of his trousers.

"Don't stop." His voice was tortured.

Her desire was coalescing inside her, a hot, hard ball of need. Regan kept circling her slippery clit. The pressure of his gaze and the look in his eyes were too much. Her back arched, electricity skating down her spine.

Regan screamed Thorin's name as she came. Her orgasm was harder than any she'd ever had before.

An almost animal sound filled the room.

Through the haze of pleasure, she saw Thorin was still watching her. He looked like he was in agony—torment in his eyes and etched on his face.

Then he turned and stumbled out. Regan shivered. Did she go after the stubborn man or not?

***

Thorin couldn't think. He slammed into his room. Need was an urgent throb through all of his body. His cock was harder and more painful than it'd ever been.

He strode across his room, feeling like he was going to burst out of his skin. He saw that his scales were out on his arms, his animal nature close to the surface.

He shoved his trousers down and took his aching cock in his hand. As he started stroking, a groan tore from his throat.

He saw Regan splayed out before him, slim fingers touching herself. All centered on that fascinating little nub that seemed to be the heart of her pleasure. He pumped his cock harder and wished it was Regan's hands on him, her mouth—

Drak. He slapped a hand against the wall to stay upright. He kept tugging, needing some sort of release, some sort of sanity in this madness.

Suddenly, he sensed her. Smelled the sweet scent of her arousal.

He felt a small hand touch his back and he went stiff. She slipped around in front of him, her white nightgown bright in the darkness. He knew she

ANNA HACKETT

shouldn't be here. He knew he should send her away.

Her hands circled his cock.

"Regan—" A tortured groan.

"Let me." She pumped him, her gaze glued to his cock. "You are so big, Thorin."

He heard the excitement in her voice and he was lost. As she worked him, his hips jerked forward.

"Drak, that...feels so good." He felt his cock pulse in her hands.

One of her hands slid down, tracing a thick vein along his cock, then back up, smoothing the fluid leaking from the tip over his length.

Then her hands were gone. He looked down and saw that she was cupping her full breasts through her nightgown. He could see the dusky shadow of her nipples through the thin fabric.

She smiled at him. How could she look both sweet and sexy at the same time? Innocent and seductress in one.

Then she was urging him toward his bed. Unable to form any words, he planted one knee on the covers.

She moved past him, lying down along the edge of the bed. She was pulling at her nightgown, but he leaned down, gripped the neckline, and tore it open with his hands.

She gasped, her teeth sinking into her bottom lip.

"I can't fuck you, Regan."

He saw her flinch and he cursed himself for being such an idiot. "I want to, but I have no control. I'm on edge. You're so small, and I'm so big. I would hurt you, and I won't do that. I would cut off my own arm with my axe before I hurt you."

Finally, she nodded, and then she moved, her hands going to her breasts again, pushing the sweet curves of them together. "Let me make you feel good. Let me taste you."

All Thorin could hear were his harsh breaths. He couldn't move, he couldn't say anything.

She reached out, guiding him toward her, until his cock slid between her soft breasts.

Sweet mother of the stars. He gulped in air.

She pushed the globes together, until they were snug around him. He moved until he was straddling her, his thighs on either side of her luscious body. The desire in her eyes was almost enough to have him spilling himself all over her.

"Move, Thorin," she urged him.

Unable to stop himself, he thrust against her, his cock sliding on her smooth skin. He moved a few times, and the next time, the swollen head of his cock touched her lips. She licked him, his cock looking so huge against her small lips.

Drak. Lost. He was lost in desire and in the other emotions mixing wildly inside him.

He kept thrusting, and started to lose his rhythm. He reached down, one hand pressed to the bed and the other tangling in her hair.

"Regan." Her name was torn out of him.

Her tongue licked at the mushroom head of his cock again, and a second later, his release hit him with the force of ten gladiators.

His seed spilled over her breasts and neck. He groaned, sensation tearing through his spine, and he kept going until there was nothing left inside him.

When he could finally think again, he dragged air into his burning lungs. He dropped down beside her on the bed, unable to tear his gaze away from her.

By the Creators, she was so pretty. He reached out and touched her plump lips, then he dragged his hand down to where his seed marked her. He dragged his fingers through it, rubbing it over her pale skin.

He saw something firing in her eyes. She liked it.

Thorin felt a desperate need to take care of her. He pushed off the bed and went into the bathroom and grabbed a warm cloth. When he returned, she was quiet, watching him as he started to wipe her clean.

"I'm not sweet and innocent."

He smiled at her. "Yes, you are. But not all the time."

She moved, getting up on her knees. Her torn nightgown fluttered around her body. "I'm a woman who knows what she wants."

He went still.

Her chin lifted. "A woman who wants you."

Gods help them both. He reached for her, fingers brushing her skin, when a knock thundered on his door, rattling it on its hinges.

"Thorin, out of bed. You and your axe are

needed." It was Raiden's deep voice. "Some crud-spawn have decided to use the storm as an excuse to cause a riot and loot houses in the area where the workers live. Some of our workers live down there and Galen wants us to check it out."

Check it out was a polite way of saying Galen wanted them to knock heads together and ensure none of their people got hurt.

Thorin's hands tightened on Regan. "I have to—"

"Go." She pulled the tattered nightgown around her. "I understand."

She was so beautiful. He cupped her jaw, pleased when she pushed into his palm. "I'll see you later."

"Promise?"

"Promise."

Chapter Ten

Regan stepped out of the shower and wrapped herself in one of the drying cloths.

After Thorin and the others had left to subdue the riot, she'd snuck back to her room. She'd been surprised to find she was tired, and had fallen into a deep, dreamless sleep.

Thorin and the others had been out the rest of the night. She'd heard them return about an hour ago.

She couldn't wait to see Thorin. What they'd done in his room... God, what they'd done.

She pushed her damp hair back and looked at herself in the round mirror above the sink in her bathroom. Across her breasts, her skin was unblemished now, but she touched it. Remembering the way he'd marked her. She smiled. She felt...happy. She tucked her hair back behind her ears. She was completely crazy over the man.

Excited to see him, she finished getting dressed, pulling on some simple slacks and a shirt from the pile of clothes Harper had given her. Now that she had money, she might do some clothes shopping in the market for some things of her own.

She headed out into the living area. Harper and a few of the house staff were busy arranging food on some plates.

Her friend looked up and smiled. She held up a plate. "Breakfast?"

Regan nodded and sat down at the table. "Where is everyone?"

"They got back late. All asleep." Harper sat down beside Regan and started eating. "But as soon as they smell food, they'll appear. Most of them seem to need a lot less sleep than we do."

"Are they all okay?" *Was Thorin all right?*

"Yep. They got the riot stamped out and the storm's dissipated."

Harper eyed her and Regan tried not to fidget.

"You look different," Harper said.

"I slept well." Regan fought to keep from blushing.

"I would have thought with the storm and what happened yesterday, you might have had trouble."

Regan dug into what looked like eggs, and freshly baked bread. "Guess I was tired." She paused a second to wonder what alien creature the eggs came from, but they were delicious, so she kept eating.

A few minutes later, Raiden appeared. The big gladiator was wearing tight, black trousers and a loose, white shirt that was undone.

He headed straight over to Harper, leaned down, and dropped a deep kiss on her lips.

Regan let out a small sigh. She wanted that. More than anything. The way Raiden cupped

Harper's cheek. The way her tough-as-nails friend leaned into the man like she knew she belonged.

A door opened and Kace entered. He looked his usual neat self, and if he was tired, he wasn't showing it.

Then Thorin strode in, and her heart clenched. He looked tired. He mumbled something and headed over to get a drink from the kitchen area.

She watched him, looking at the way his trousers hugged his firm ass. She couldn't believe he'd been standing over her, naked, just a few hours ago.

"The next time some idiots get the idea to go rioting, I suggest we leave them to it." Saff stomped in. She had dark circles under her eyes. "I need a hot cup of *rica* with a shot of stimulant in it."

Thorin came over and dropped down into the seat beside Regan. She was so blazingly aware of him. She wanted to say something or touch him.

"Sleep well?"

"I did."

He seemed focused on drinking the coffee-like drink the others called *rica*. But then she felt a touch on her hair and realized he was stroking the back of her head. Something in her chest bloomed.

Everyone sat down, talking and diving into eating plates of food filled mountain high. Regan sat there, surrounded by all this muscle and toughness, and for the first time in her life, she felt like she belonged.

The door opened and Galen strode in. She noticed all the others pause and look up.

Galen dropped into a chair at the head of the table. Lore sauntered over from the kitchen area and set a mug of *rica* down in front of the imperator.

"I'm guessing this isn't just a friendly morning visit," Raiden said.

Galen shook his head. "My informant got back to me with the list of people at the Thraxians' private sale. That information, combined with the attempt to snatch Regan yesterday, has given us enough to pinpoint where Rory is being held."

Regan clenched her hands together, remembering those terrible moments when Kace had been hurt and she'd been snatched. Thorin's big hand closed over both of hers.

"It is the Vorn," Galen said.

"Damn," Thorin said. There were grumbles from the rest of the gladiators.

Regan's skin turned icy with dread. "Who are they?"

"They are wild and...crazy. In the arena, it is hard to predict a Vorn's fighting techniques. And their imperator..."

She gripped his arm. "Yes?"

"The Vorn like to collect rare things," Thorin said.

Galen nodded. "Their imperator is known far and wide for collecting unique specimens of plants, animals, and people."

"Why would he try to take me?"

"I suspect he wants a matching set," Galen said darkly. "I met with him this morning."

Already? Regan straightened. "Will they trade her, or let you fight for her?"

A muscle in Galen's jaw ticked. "They won't even admit they have her."

Regan's shoulders fell.

"I had to make sure that they saw this didn't bother me." Galen's cool blue eye looked at Regan. "If they knew—"

She nodded. "I know. They'd make things more difficult."

"The Vorn will have her in their collection room." Raiden rested his elbows on the table. "I've never seen it, but I've heard whispers about the place. It's meant to be something, with amazing plant life and animals."

"It's just another prison," Regan whispered.

Under the table, Thorin gripped her thigh. That strong touch was enough to anchor her.

"Can we break in?" Harper asked.

Regan suspected that due to their secret rescue missions, they all knew the strengths and weaknesses of every house in the arena.

Galen shook his head. "Security at the House of Vorn is top-of-the-line. They like to protect their collection. They have sensors, laser systems, alarms. And those are the things that I know about."

Lore gave a thoughtful nod. "I've heard it can only be shut down from the inside."

Regan pressed back into her chair. How the hell would they get Rory out of there?

Around her, the gladiators erupted into

discussion, making suggestions and discarding ideas. Regan turned the dilemma over in her head, analyzing it like a science problem.

"What we need is to lure them out," Regan blurted out.

Silence fell around the table. Everyone's gazes turned toward her.

She tried not to fidget. "We need to lure them out by offering them something they really want. And then get them to take that something back into their house. Something that can shut down their security from the inside."

"A Trojan Horse," Harper murmured.

"A what?" Thorin demanded.

Regan swallowed. "An old Earth legend. About a horse filled with enemy soldiers that was taken back inside a fortified city."

Galen stared at her, his fingers drumming on the table. "Lure them out with what?"

Regan was careful not to look at Thorin. "Something—or rather, someone—they can't resist."

Thorin's fingers tightened on her thigh. "No."

Regan lifted her chin. "Lure them out with me."

***

Anger. Gut-churning anger.

Thorin had felt the hot edge of fury before, but what he felt now was a hundred times stronger.

Added to his tiredness, his barely sated desire, and the sting of his torn knuckles from knocking heads together in the riot, he wasn't finding much patience.

He saw his friends looking at him, and he shook his head.

"No. We will not use her as bait and let them take her."

He stared into her pretty eyes, but in his mind, he saw her spread out before him, his cock pressed to her lips. It was burned on his brain.

He stood, conscious that the room was silent.

Regan stood, setting her shoulders back. "I want Rory back. I want her out of captivity. This is the only way. I go in, disable the security from the inside, and you come and get us."

The anger surged, like a wild beast. She wanted to walk into danger. He swept his arm across the table. Plates and glasses hit the stone floor, smashing into tiny pieces. He saw Regan wince, but she stood her ground.

Thorin heard Raiden sigh.

"Been a while since he lost it so much he broke plates," Lore said lazily.

"Shush," Saff said. "Or he'll break your nose."

Thorin ignored them and rounded on Regan. "You will not risk yourself like that."

"I have to do this," she said calmly.

"So, you want us to sell you? You want to end up back in the cage?"

He saw her flinch, shadows moving through her eyes, and Thorin hated himself for hurting her. He reached out and grabbed her shoulders. "I forbid it."

The shadows fled. "You forbid it? I've had lots of people in my life demanding I do this or that. Things that suit them, not me." She poked the center of his chest. "I won't let you do the same."

"Regan—"

"I need your support, Thorin. I need you at my back."

Drak. He turned away, putting his hands behind his head. It went against everything in him to let her put herself in danger. He felt like the terrible tension in his body was going to break him.

"We'll all be there for you, Regan," Harper said.

"We'll all be there to ensure she stays safe," Raiden added.

Thorin stared at the wall, trying to find another way to do this. He wanted to pull her into his arms, carry her away and keep her safe. But that would condemn her cousin to a terrible fate, and Regan would never forgive him.

"Please, Thorin."

Her quiet words cut through him. Damn these Earth women for being so damned courageous.

Finally, he dropped his arms and turned, his anger going cold. "You will have a tracker implanted. I won't lose you if something goes wrong."

Regan opened her mouth to object, but Galen nodded. "Absolutely."

"And after they purchase her, we go in straightaway. She won't be in a cage for more than an hour."

Again, Galen nodded.

Regan moved over to Thorin, pressing her fingers lightly against his chest. "Thank you."

He reached out and yanked her into his chest. He couldn't get her close enough.

"So what happens next?" Harper asked.

Galen stood. "We need to organize a private party to auction Regan at. Something flashy." His gaze turned inward. "I think I'll touch base with Rillian at the Dark Nebula Casino."

Thorin knew that the Dark Nebula was the classiest and wealthiest of all the casinos in Kor Magna. And its owner was a very scary, very wealthy man.

"Who's this Rillian?" Regan asked.

"A powerful man," Galen said. "He appeared from nowhere fifteen years ago and turned a small casino into the wealthiest enterprise on the planet. He has his fingers in a lot of things, and he owes me a marker."

"Rillian will be able to arrange a party that the Vorn won't be able to turn down," Raiden said.

Regan nodded. "Okay. Let's do it."

Galen's gaze swept the room. "Consider it done. But for now, you all have a private exhibition match against the House of Nalax to prepare for. The son of a wealthy finance lord from Maton II has a birthday."

There were groans from the gladiators.

Galen's face remained impassive. "He's paying a lot of money to see you guys beat the House of Nalax. Don't disappoint him."

As Galen left, Thorin held Regan tight. So small,

and delicate—but he knew looks could be very deceiving.

The anger in him wasn't gone. Instead, it was just waiting for its chance to pounce. And he'd be happy to pound out his frustration on some gladiators in the arena.

Chapter Eleven

Regan watched Thorin land another bone-jarring blow to the gladiator he was fighting. She winced.

The private exhibition fight was in full swing.

Tonight, Thorin had forgone his axe and was wearing heavy, metal knuckledusters on his hands. Clearly, he was determined to work off his anger at her decision in the arena.

He got in another hit before he charged forward, knocking over several opposing gladiators.

This exhibition fight was scaled down, and in a small private arena. She glanced over at the sponsor box that protruded out over the sand floor, and studied the wealthy-looking man and his entourage, all of them dressed in gaudy colors and drinking and laughing as the fight raged beneath them.

The House of Nalax had a mix of tough gladiators, but Regan noticed one who seemed to be smaller and less experienced than the others. He'd fumbled his sword numerous times.

She wasn't surprised that the House of Galen gladiators weren't engaging him.

Thorin swung at some more gladiators, flesh hitting flesh. Then he spun around to face another

Nalax gladiator, only to discover the undersized gladiator cowering before him. Thorin eyed him for a second, before he pushed the man aside and went after another gladiator.

He was angry, but he was still a badass protector. Her chest felt as tight as a rock. He was upset at her, hurting, and she was to blame.

"So...you and Thorin worked things out."

Regan glanced at Harper, who sat beside her, munching on some *mahiz*.

Regan shrugged. "It's complicated."

Harper snorted. "It always is when men are involved."

Regan fought back a smile. "You'd think the fact that we've been dragged halfway across the galaxy might have made things a bit different."

"Right. You think that meeting an alpha-male, alien gladiator on the outer rim of the galaxy would equal no complications."

Well, when Harper put it like that... "It's just that life seems simpler in the arena. Train, fight, win. Once you have your freedom, do as you please."

Harper's gaze was on the fight. "They're heroes, Regan. Loved by the crowd." Her gaze now moved to the shouting spectators. "But the face they show the fans, it's a façade. They rarely show anyone who they really are. All of them ended up here for different reasons—hard, dark reasons. They are tough, relentless fighters...but it's just one side of them. And they only let the people they care about see their true selves."

Once again, Regan watched Thorin slamming hard punches into an opponent. "He's holding a lot of darkness inside him. A lot of hurt."

Harper squeezed Regan's shoulder. "Raiden is, too. Just because we've fallen in love doesn't make that magically disappear. But I've seen that...his load's lightened a little." She smiled, her gaze finding her man. "I like to think that I did that."

Regan's throat tightened. "I think I've just added to Thorin's load." She watched him, as he fought like a man possessed. "And he refuses to show me his hurt. I feel like he's hiding something."

"He's afraid for you. I am, too."

"Harper, I—"

Her friend nodded. "Have to do this. I know. I understand. I want Rory back safe, too. I just wish you didn't have to risk yourself to do it."

"You think she's okay?"

"I've never met a tougher woman than Rory. That woman takes crap from no one."

Regan nodded. She always admired her confident cousin, but Regan knew what captivity could do to you. How it could slowly break you down.

"Galen's making the arrangements for the party," Harper said.

Regan took a deep breath. "Good." She wouldn't lie. She was terrified.

"You have all of us there for you. Including Thorin, even if he's pissed off."

Suddenly, the crowd gasped.

Regan swiveled and saw Thorin was fighting

with a gladiator almost as tall as he was. The rival gladiator was holding long knives. He slashed out and opened a cut across Thorin's chest. A cry tangled in Regan's throat. *Move faster, Thorin.* She watched as the gladiator sliced him again.

She saw that Thorin was smiling.

Regan jumped to her feet, her hands curling around the railing. "He's letting that gladiator hurt him."

Then Thorin charged.

He attacked the gladiator hard. The other man's knives landed in the sand, along with the blood splatter from Thorin's vicious blows. She saw his scales had appeared across his chest and arms. Regan looked away, sucking in air. This was her fault. She looked back, and as the gladiator tumbled backward onto the sand, Thorin followed him down, never faltering in his hits.

Raiden and Nero hauled Thorin off the man.

A siren wailed, and the announcer called the fight over. Since this was an exhibition match, there was no winner.

Raiden and Nero pulled a struggling Thorin out of the arena.

"I…have to go," she said.

Harper nodded. "Take care of him."

***

Thorin relished the sting of the cuts on his chest. He was covered in sweat and blood.

"What in drak's name were you thinking?" Raiden bit out.

Thorin stayed silent.

Raiden cursed. "I know you're upset about the plan, but that doesn't mean you beat some poor bastard half to death in an exhibition match."

"What if it was Harper?" Thorin's words came out like projectiles. "What if she was going to be sold to the Vorn?"

He saw Raiden's face go tight.

Thorin shook his head. "Hell, it's not even the same. Harper can protect herself, Regan can't."

Raiden crossed his arms over his chest. "She's smart, clever. You need to trust her."

The emotions writhing in his chest were too much. "This...is stirring me. I can't find any control."

The other man's face turned serious. "Your...heritage is rising up."

"Yes." Thorin stared at the scales on his arms. They were just a warning. He stalked off. Anger and fear were twisting inside him. Hell, fear. When was the last time he'd been afraid?

He thought back, and could remember those moments in his brother's ship, coming in to land at Kor Magna. His brother hadn't said a word, but Thorin had known what was going to happen. He'd been a battle-hardened warrior and he'd still been terrified.

But the first time he'd been forced into the arena, he'd vowed never to be afraid again.

At first, he'd embraced and let loose the animal

side that lived inside him. Then, with Raiden's help, he'd learned to control it.

Now, he was losing control of it, and he had no idea what to do. Thorin stomped into the House of Galen, watching workers scatter out of his way. He stalked through the living area and into his room.

Then he stopped and stared.

There were little candles everywhere. Regan was standing beside his bed in a simple blue dress. The outfit hugged all her curves and dipped low enough at the neck to show a hint of cleavage.

They stared at each other. Beside her was a plain wooden chair, and on a small stand a bowl of steaming-hot water.

"Sit," she said quietly.

He didn't move.

Her eyes flashed. "Sit."

He dropped into the chair. She reached out, her fingers brushing over the fastenings of his harness. She took her time unbuckling it and slipping it off his chest. Then she grabbed his left hand, her fingers moving over the bloodstained knuckledusters. He almost snatched his hand away, but sensing his thoughts, her grip tightened. He watched as she pulled them off, and then lifted his right hand and did the same. It seemed wrong to see the blood smeared on her fingers.

Then, he felt her fingers in a feather-light touch over his torn knuckles.

She let his hand go, reached over to the bowl, and wrung out a cloth. She started cleaning his wounds. He watched as the candlelight flickered over her skin, turning it golden. She wordlessly cleaned his right hand and then his left.

After rinsing the cloth again, she started dabbing at the cuts on his chest. She made a clucking sound. "You shouldn't have let them hurt you."

Her touch was driving Thorin crazy. Her scent was seeping into his senses, so deep he knew he'd never get it out. He felt his scales flicker along his arms. He felt like a beast in rut. He wanted to tear her clothes off, push her down onto the ground—

Far too easily, he could see the two of them tangled on the bed as he drove inside her. He stiffened. She deserved better than a beast.

She touched a deep cut on his shoulder and he made a hissing sound. She took her time, being careful as she cleaned it. Then she leaned down and pressed her lips to it. So quick and light he barely registered it before she was standing again.

"Go in and shower. After, I'll put some of my med gel on you."

Thorin didn't protest. He couldn't deny this woman had some sort of power over him. He went into his bathroom, shed the rest of his clothes, and stepped under the water. He didn't linger in the shower, and he kept it cold. His hands clenched into fists against the stone tiles. He needed to find some control. He needed to send her away.

He dried himself with a few careless swipes of the drying cloth. He wrapped the damp fabric around his waist, and headed back into the bedroom.

She waved him back to the chair, and he sat down again. Then, her small hands were smoothing med gel on the cuts on his chest.

"I don't deserve this," he grumbled.

Regan eyed him. "Everyone deserves to be taken care of now and then. Even big, brooding gladiators."

She went back to her task. She kept stroking her fingers and the gel across his skin, and his cock swelled. She pressed into him as she reached up to the cuts on his shoulders, her full breasts pressing against him.

His hands clenched on her hips. "Regan."

She must have heard the strain in his voice. She tossed the med gel aside, resting her hands on his shoulders. "Take what you need, Thorin."

"What?" He frowned at her.

"Haven't you realized yet that I'm yours?"

His? No one had ever been his. The people he thought he'd loved had tossed him away.

"I'm not going anywhere," she whispered.

With a groan, he tugged her forward. She landed in his lap, straddling him. He liked the little gasp she made.

Then Thorin reached up, gripped the top of her dress, and tore it open. Her breasts spilled out.

"Thorin! You have to stop tearing my clothes."

He froze. "Don't you like it?"

Her mouth opened, then closed. "Well..."

He grinned. She liked it. He pulled her forward, sucking one pink nipple between his lips. Her hands moved up, clamping onto his head. She moaned.

He kept sucking and licking. Then he moved across to the other globe, teasing that pretty nipple.

Holding her like this, touching her, tasting her, she felt like his redemption. This lush woman who looked at him like he was good and light. She was shifting against him now, making small, urgent sounds.

He lifted his head and touched his mouth to hers.

He'd never been a kisser—it was always too intimate, too slow. But he loved the taste of Regan. He thrust his tongue inside her mouth, wanting to explore every part of her, taste every part of her.

"I'm burning up." Her words were a husky whisper.

He reached down and slid one hand under her dress. He moved along her thigh, until he found the damp heat of her. She wasn't wearing any underwear. He ran his fingers through her folds. "You're soaked."

She blushed. "For you."

He wanted to hear her come. He'd watched her pleasure herself just that morning, but he hadn't had the chance to touch her, to be the one that made her come. He parted her folds and slid one thick finger inside her.

Her moan was long and loud. Drak, she was tight. For a moment, he wondered if he'd fit inside her. He moved up, finding that intriguing little nub he'd watched her play with.

"Oh." She jerked. "Yes."

"What is this called?" He circled the sensitive flesh.

"Clitoris." Her voice was breathy. "My clit." She frowned, curiosity shining in his little scientist's eyes. "You haven't...um...seen—"

"Usually the sensitive places are inside the females."

He pumped his finger inside her again. He needed to make sure she was ready for him.

Her mouth opened, her hands digging into his shoulders. "I've always thought it should have been on the inside, too. That would make life much easier."

"I like you just as you are, Regan." The way she was moving, grinding on his hand, told him that she liked his touch. He carefully worked a second finger inside her.

"Yes, Thorin. Make me come."

He loved hearing her talk like that. Dirty words said in such a prim, proper tone. He moved his thumb until he found her clit again. He watched her move, moaning, and he desperately wanted to know what her clit felt like on his tongue. *Later.* He made the promise to himself. For now, he pressed down on it in slick circles.

"Yes." She was riding against his hand, trying to find her release. Then she gasped and arched her back. As she cried out, he'd never seen anything prettier.

Her head flopped down against his shoulder, her quick breathing echoing in his ear. "I need you inside me, Thorin. Please don't make me wait anymore."

He couldn't. He'd told himself a thousand times to stay away from her, but he couldn't stop the need, and he couldn't find the strength to push her away.

He shoved the drying cloth around his hips to the side, freeing his straining cock. It was harder than it had ever been, pointing straight up. Then he yanked the remains of her dress off her hips.

"You're in charge." His voice sounded so hoarse it was hard to make out his words. He wanted to push her back on the big bed, cover her with his body.

But he wouldn't risk hurting her this first time. He had to take care of her.

He curled his hands around her waist, and lifted her up. She touched his face, his lips. Was she memorizing what he looked like? No one had ever stared at his rough face with such wonder. He wasn't handsome like Kace, or rugged like Raiden. She leaned forward and again they kissed—rough, edgy, her teeth sinking into his lip. He slid his hands down to cup her ass, his hands clenching on the sweet globes.

"I've got a big bottom," she said quietly.

He stroked her flesh. "You're perfect." He groaned.

She was moving against him now, each shimmy rubbing his cock against the damp flesh between her thighs.

Then she reached down and gripped his cock.

She pushed up a little, pressing her other hand against his shoulder. She moved until the thick head of him was lodged at her slick opening, then her eyes met his. She lowered herself down.

Drak. She was warm and wet and so damn tight.

The fat, swollen head of him slid inside her and he watched as she bit her lip.

"You're so big," she whimpered.

Don't stop. "Take your time." The words cost him. He wanted to slam inside her, to throw her on the bed and take her.

She kept lowering herself down, and he felt her stretching around him.

"So full." Her mouth rounded into a perfect *O.*

Thorin gritted his teeth. *Control.* He needed control. "I'm hurting you."

"No. It feels good." Her hand touched his jaw, forcing his head up. "Take me."

Unable to stop himself, he slammed his hips up, filling her, his cock lodged deep.

Her nails bit into his shoulders and she cried out.

He froze. "You're too tight."

"No." She moved her hips, finding some secret rhythm. "I like the way you fill me up."

She started lifting herself up and down, riding him hard. His hands flexed on her ass and he growled, the last of his conscious thought slipping away.

Mine. Always mine. A greedy, animal echo from deep within him.

As his control snapped, he thrust into her, determined to make this woman his in every way.

Chapter Twelve

They were both slippery with sweat, grinding against each other. Regan was panting, hovering on the edge of another orgasm. She was so close, but she couldn't quite get there.

She was so full and stretched. Thorin kept working her up and down on his massive cock, and she was a trembling mess.

"Thorin." She wasn't sure what she was asking for, but he seemed to know.

"You need my help, sweetness?" One rough hand slid between their bodies. "I'll help you."

He found her clit and she whimpered. As he rubbed it, electricity shot through her, building so bright she felt a lick of fear.

"Come on my cock, Regan. Let me feel you squeezing me."

Hearing that raspy voice saying her name set her off. She screamed, exquisite waves of pleasure slamming into her like a full-body blow.

Thorin surged up to his feet, holding her tight, keeping himself lodged inside her. He took a few steps to the bed. She was still in the throes of her orgasm as he lay her down, his weight coming down on top of her. She loved the heavy feel of him.

He thrust in, deeper than before. She screamed again and this time he took complete control. He was slamming into her over and over, until an animal growl was torn from his throat.

"That's me inside you, Regan. You're mine."

"Yes!"

He pulled out, staying with just the head of his cock lodged inside her. "Are you mine, Regan?" He pushed inside her. "Is this all mine?"

He was straining above her, his muscles tense, his face harsh.

"Yours," she murmured. She'd never felt so safe, so consumed, so right, as she did with this man.

He pushed deep, holding himself there as he came inside her.

When he collapsed on her, she felt him readying himself to move. Regan clamped her arms and legs around him. "Don't go."

"I'm too heavy." He shifted to the side and pulled her in close, his cock still inside her. "I'm not going anywhere."

Regan sighed. Lazily, she leaned forward to press a kiss against his slick chest. "I've never had sex like that."

A rough hand stroked down her spine, before coming to rest on her ass. "I don't think anyone has had sex like that."

She smiled against his skin. He was so big, hard, and tough, but he could still be sweet. He looked down at her, his face relaxed, but somehow fierce at the same time. She wondered if her gladiator was ever truly at peace.

"I hated seeing you get hurt," she told him.

His arms tightened around her. "I was stupid to take the emotions into the arena. Raiden is always reminding us to keep a cool head."

"You let that gladiator hurt you."

Thorin pulled in a breath. "When I first came here, I was so angry. At my brother, my family, the situation. I'd dedicated my life to being a warrior for my people, and they threw that back at me. I found fighting helped me find some control. And when I got hurt, the pain helped me as well."

She made a small sound. "You need the pain?"

"Not anymore. It doesn't arouse me, or anything. There are some gladiators I know who get turned on by it. I was young and out of control."

"You were young, abandoned, and hurting."

"Tough gladiators don't like to admit that." He drew in a deep breath. "It was more than that."

She sensed the seriousness in his tone. "Tell me, Thorin." She stroked a hand down his arm. "It has to do with your scales."

He cursed under his breath. When he tried to pull away, she held on tight.

"Tell me."

"My species is the Sirrush. We're big, strong, have enhanced senses. We were warriors."

That described her gladiator perfectly. "Okay."

"But centuries ago, our planet was invaded by another alien species." His jaw worked. "They were a wild, brutish race. Scaled, wild, and vicious."

Regan fought to keep her emotions off her face.

"They raped and plundered until they were

finally defeated. But every now and then, a Sirrush child will show throwback characteristics of those invaders. A beast living inside them." His gaze bored into her. "I am a monster."

Regan traced lazy circles on his chest, over the hard planes of muscle. "I love your scales, Thorin. I don't see a monster."

"Sometimes I lose control—"

"Lots of people do. It doesn't make you an animal."

"You don't understand. When I got here...I was an animal. My family used me as a warrior, a weapon, and then when..."

When he'd gotten too dangerous, they'd abandoned him. She kept touching him. Something warned her that Thorin would need her to show him that she accepted him just as he was. Words wouldn't be enough.

"It's hard to be alone. No one to lean on." She remembered being in her cell. So completely alone.

"Do not think of the Thraxians." His hands slid over hers. "You aren't alone anymore."

No. She had Harper, and this big, tough alien who had finally let her sneak past his hard shell. "I know you're angry about the plan—"

He cupped her chin. "Tonight, it's just you and me. I don't want to think about tomorrow yet."

She nodded. "I like the sound of that. So, what will we do?"

"Well, I was thinking we'd take a shower together."

She shivered. Imagining his rough, soapy hands

rubbing over her skin. "That sounds nice."

"Then I'll lay you out and lick between your legs until you come."

She gasped. "Oh."

She heard him laugh. "You like the sound of that, huh, sweetness? I'm also planning to have my cock deep inside you all night."

All night? She wasn't sure if she was excited, horrified, or impressed. Okay, she was excited.

"I'm going to take you every way I know," he said, his voice turning to a growl.

Oh, boy.

When he scooped her up and carried her toward the bathroom, Regan knew she was in for a long, wild night.

***

"I've been looking for a guinea pig to try my new batch of liniment on."

Thorin finished wiping the drying cloth across his chest and looked over at Regan. She was sitting on the edge of his bed, wearing one of his shirts. It was far too large and falling off one shoulder, baring smooth skin. It was late. He'd taken the time to sneak out to find some food for them to refuel. He'd gorged on her for hours, but now, seeing her bare legs and shoulders, and messy sunshine hair, he felt something stir inside him. A hunger not yet satisfied.

"Guinea pig?" he asked.

"Oh, a cute, little, fluffy animal on Earth."

139

He blinked. "You think I am like a cute, little, fluffy animal?"

She smiled. "No. Guinea pigs used to be used as test subjects before we found other ways to test products. I want you to be my test subject." She held up a small pot. "Lie facedown on the bed. Let me rub this on you."

He frowned. "It better not smell like flowers."

A happy smile floated on her lips. "No flowers." She opened the pot and a strong, citrus scent filled the room.

He'd been so focused on his own anger and fear about using Regan as bait. Now that he saw her, flushed and relaxed, he realized she'd been worrying, too.

And he'd been making her burden greater. He realized he'd do anything to keep that smile on her face.

He lay down on the bed, resting his head on his forearms. She moved up close to him, and he felt the cool liniment touch his skin. She started rubbing his back with firm strokes. She had surprisingly strong hands. It felt good.

And she showed no hesitation about touching him. He'd bared his past, and while he knew she truly couldn't understand it, she didn't seem bothered at all.

"I tried a few different mixtures, but I think this one's the best." She kneaded his muscles, and rattled on about the benefits of her liniment. The things she'd tried that hadn't worked, and how she'd come to her current formulation.

He smiled. She clearly loved her work. His woman was smart.

His woman?

"Hey, you tensed up." She moved her hands in a soothing stroke up his spine. "Just relax."

Did he want Regan to be his? *Yes.* He still wasn't sure he was good enough for her. If she ever truly saw what lived inside him, she'd run screaming.

Her hands paused. "Thorin, your scales are showing."

"It's a sign of...strong emotion." He felt her stillness.

"What are you feeling right now?"

"Happy."

He waited for her to say something, but instead, he felt her move and press a kiss to the base of his neck.

"Me, too. When I got taken, happiness seemed so far away. Just a distant, impossible dream. Hell, even before I got taken, I wasn't happy."

Thorin turned his head. "Why?"

"My parents...they wanted me to marry, not work, and definitely not go into space."

They wanted to stifle her? "Why would they do that?"

"They had different beliefs. They couldn't understand my deep passion for my work. I was never good enough for them."

He gripped her thigh. "That is their failing, not yours."

She cleared her throat. "Okay, big guy. Roll over.

I'm going to rub your chest next."

Thorin turned over, stretching his shoulders. His muscles felt loose and relaxed. "The liniment is good."

"Thanks."

As he resettled, he ensured the cloth covering his hips fell away. He watched as Regan's gaze drifted down his chest, loving that eager, hungry look in her eyes. Then her gaze came to rest on his rock-hard cock.

Now her eyes widened. "Thorin." She licked her lips. "How can you be ready again?"

"By looking at you." He raised one hand, tugging at the shirt, pulling it open. "This shirt is mine."

"Don't tear it." She let out a laugh. "We won't have any clothes left at the rate you're going." She set the pot of liniment on the bedside table. Then she pulled the shirt over her head.

Now it was Thorin's turn to look at her with hunger. All those gorgeous curves of hers.

"Come here," he growled. He was suddenly very hungry.

He pulled her up, listening to her husky cries as he positioned her across his body. When he settled her knees on either side of his head, he saw her cheeks go pink.

"Thorin, I'm not sure abou—"

He gripped her knees, looking up at the pink folds above him. Without warning her, he licked her.

She jerked. "Oh, God. That's so good."

Thorin set to work eating her. He licked, sucked,

and stabbed his tongue inside her. He loved the taste of her and he knew he'd never get enough of it. She started making little cries, her sweet center grinding against his face. He loved how uninhibited she was in his arms, and he loved the sounds she made as he pleasured her.

He kept going, feeling her thighs tensing. He found that small clit that was the epicenter of her pleasure and lavished it with attention. He could feel her release getting closer. More than anything, he wanted to hear her cry his name as she came.

He sucked deeply, lapping at her again, and her back locked, her body shuddering above his. The sound of his name torn from her throat echoed in his room.

She collapsed down on top of him, and he shifted her so she was curled up on his chest. She was still shivering a little against him. He stroked her back, breathed her in.

"I've lost track of how many times I've orgasmed," she said. "I'm pretty sure you're not supposed to come this many times in one day."

He smiled against her hair. "I don't think there's a rule."

She shifted, her legs sliding against his, bumping into his cock. She raised her head, and he saw a light ignite in her eyes.

She didn't say anything, just slid off him and onto her knees by his hips. Then she reached out and wrapped her hands around him, smoothing those slim fingers along his heavy cock.

Drak. Thorin's stomach muscles tightened. "Regan."

"I want to make you feel good." She pumped his cock in her hand. "I want to make you feel how you made me feel."

He wasn't sure he had the control for this. Then she leaned down and sucked the swollen head of his cock between her lips.

He forced himself not to surge up. There was no way she could take all of him in her mouth, but what she was doing still felt good. She was sliding her tongue along him, and the image of her lips on him was enough to drive him insane.

"Regan." He tangled one hand in her hair.

"I've imagined this." She moved both her hands around the engorged base of his cock. "The other night, I only got in a few licks. It wasn't enough."

He groaned. "I've imagined it, too."

She looked up at him. "What do you want?"

"Suck my cock, Regan."

She made a hungry sound, one of her hands sliding to press on his thigh for leverage. He felt her fingers digging into his skin. She leaned down and sucked him as deep as she could.

"Sweetness—" Hell, he was coming apart.

She never took her gaze off him. Staring down at his sweet, sexy Regan with her lips around his cock was just too much.

"I'm going to come." He was so close.

She sucked harder.

With a shout, Thorin came. He felt his release pumping out of him, pleasure an explosion through his body.

Regan swallowed everything down, and as he collapsed back on the bed, she slowly looked at him.

Thorin yanked her up. "You're too good for me."

"Stop saying that. I've wanted to do that for so long." Her hands moved over his chest. "Ever since I first saw you, I've been having all these naughty thoughts. Of my big, tough, protective gladiator."

He pulled her close. Regan saw more in him than he did. She saw things that he liked, that he wanted to be, but he still wasn't certain they were really there.

***

"Oh, Thorin. More."

Regan was on her belly, pressed into the pillows on the bed. Thorin was sliding into her from behind. His thick cock stretched her, moving in and out ruthlessly.

Daylight shone through the window, and over the tangled sheets on the bed. She was a little sore from everything they'd done during the night and the morning, and in this position, he felt even bigger.

His fingers were digging into her hips, his thrusting cock moving in and out of her. The pleasure was indescribable. She felt wild and wanton.

She shoved back against him. She needed more. She needed something. She heard him groan, and the next time he thrust deep, she came. She turned her head, biting the pillow to muffle her scream.

He powered into her again and then he grabbed her roughly, slamming home, roaring as he came deep inside her.

He dropped down beside her on the bed. He touched her cheek, then pushed her hair off her face.

"I was rough. Are you okay?"

She gave him a lazy smile. "I think I can only move my lips. Everything else is limp."

He smiled. It almost softened his hard face. "You'll need to move soon. Galen's having dresses for the party delivered, and they should be here at any time." His smile dissolved, his face hardening.

She reached out and cupped his cheek. "Thorin, I know—"

"Shh." He gripped her shoulders. "I know you need to do this. I may have no blood family, but I have my friends. Brothers not by the blood in our veins, but by the blood of our fights together. I would fight to free them, do whatever I had to do." He took a deep breath. "I wish you didn't have to risk yourself, but I will be there the entire time. I will have your back."

Regan's heart melted a little. "Thank you."

There was a knock at the door.

With a squeak, Regan jumped up. She was lying here naked with more than a few stubble burns and bruises all over her, and Thorin's seed drying on her thighs. "I need to shower."

He grinned at her. "Not so limp now." He reached out, stroking his hand down her side.

She smacked his hand away. "Shoo." She took one step to the bathroom, then paused, her gaze sliding over him. "Clothes on, gladiator. No one sees you naked anymore but me."

He shot her a wide, satisfied grin. "Sure thing, sweetness."

Regan closed the door to the bathroom and stepped in under the big shower. The water fell down like a waterfall and she poured some liquid soap in her hands. She let her hands drift over her body, cupping breasts that Thorin had thoroughly licked and sucked. She slid her fingers down her belly, washing away the come he'd spilled there. Next, she moved her hands between her legs, where he'd taken her over and over again.

She smiled to herself. Thorin was hers. She could see that he cared about her.

Once Rory was free, everything would be right in Regan's life. She might have lost Earth and the only family she'd ever known, but she knew she could make a life for herself here. A good one.

When she came out of the shower wrapped in a drying cloth, she saw three dresses hanging up against the wall. They were all beautiful, but seeing them made her throat go tight.

The party was this evening. She'd be up for sale, even if it was a ruse, and these dresses were just a pretty version of chains.

The dresses were all pale colors—white, blush pink, and baby blue. One had a halter-style top. One was goddess-style, leaving one shoulder bare. The final one was strapless. All were long and flowing, but cut to fall close to her body. She reached out and fingered the fabric.

Thorin came up behind her. A big, protective presence.

"I'm nervous," she said.

"Good. It'll keep you sharp." His arms came around her, pulling her close to him. "You'll do great a job. And I won't be far away."

She leaned into him. "I don't know which one to wear."

"Wear the blue. It looks good against your skin and that golden hair of yours."

The blue had the halter top that would tie at the back of her neck. It was pretty.

Thorin's hands drifted over her hips. "And while you're wearing it, think of me pushing the folds of that long skirt up and sliding inside you."

That made her smile. Knowing that he'd be close by made her feel better about this. She knew Thorin would come for her, no matter what.

"They also left some…paints." He waved at her face.

"Makeup?"

He nodded. "And things for your hair. If you need help, a house worker can aid you."

"I can manage."

Then he turned her. He held something in the palm of his hand.

"What's that?" It was a small, black square.

"It is a disruptor device. It will disrupt the Vorn's security and allow us access to the house."

She took it. "What do I do with it?"

"Once you are inside, just press the button on it and hide it somewhere."

Sounded easy enough. She tucked it into the folds of her dress.

Thorin held out something else. It was a small blue dot the size of her thumb nail.

"The tracker. It has to be implanted under your skin."

Her stomach balked. One part of her wanted it, for security. The other hated the idea that people could monitor her every move.

"No tracker, no plan." His tone was unbending.

She nodded.

"Good girl. If you're ready, I'll get one of the Hermia healers to come and put it in. It won't hurt. I promise."

She nodded. She trusted him completely.

Chapter Thirteen

As Regan entered the living area, everyone looked up at her. She fought the urge to grip the fabric of her dress as a distraction.

Harper hurried over. "You look beautiful."

"All the better to sell me to the highest bidder."

Harper's hands tightened on Regan's arms. "You don't have to do this."

"Yes, I do. For Rory."

Harper was quiet for a moment. "For Rory. And for Madeline when we finally get a lead on her location." Harper cleared her throat. "Want to tell me about spending the entire night locked in Thorin's room?"

Regan fought to control her blush. "No."

Harper leaned closer. "In case you weren't aware, you're a screamer."

Oh, God. Now Regan's cheeks flamed. "I...I..."

Her friend grinned. "So, it was good?

Regan managed a nod.

"On a scale from one to ten?"

"About a hundred."

Harper's smile widened. "Good."

Raiden strode in. Regan got the pleasure of watching Harper flush, her gaze tracking her lover.

He was far more dressed up than Regan had ever seen him. He wore a slick shirt in dark gray, tucked into black leather trousers. His muscles were covered, but there was no mistaking him for anything but the badass gladiator he was.

"Regan?"

She turned and saw Lore standing nearby.

"I'm not involved in tonight's mission, but I wanted to give you something." He held out his hand.

She studied his long-fingered palm. Nothing. "What? Is this one of your illusions?"

He used his other hand and peeled a small, flesh-colored square off his hand. "No. This is a high-tech explosive. You can place it on any solid metal surface. It has a time-delayed micro-explosion that will slowly eat away at the metal."

She took it gingerly, leaned down, and pressed it onto her ankle. "It's not going to blow up in my face?"

He smiled. "No." He handed her a second explosive square and then flicked a finger at her chin. "Good luck. See you when you get back."

Thorin appeared. "Ready?" His hungry eyes were taking her in and Regan did the same. He wore a similar outfit to Raiden's, but his gray shirt had no sleeves, showcasing the bulge of his biceps.

"Ready."

Later, when she stepped through the grand entrance of the Dark Nebula Casino, her hands twisted anxiously in the fabric of her dress.

The casino was a blur to her. There were slick,

black walls decorated with interesting artwork, and elegant vases filled with amazing, exotic flowers. She looked up and for a second, her attention snagged on the ceiling. Wow. It was lit up like a multi-hued nebula—stars twinkling, colors shifting.

But then the massive throb of sound, the blinking lights of gambling machines, and the throng of people inside overwhelmed her. There were crowds of aliens—both humanoid and not—all hunched over various tables, playing games she didn't recognize.

Her dress whispered around her body, and her wrist ached a little where the tracker had been implanted, even though there was no sign of it from the outside. Galen stood by her side, and behind her Raiden and Thorin loomed. The men were all alert, their gazes scanning around.

"This way." Galen urged her on with a gentle touch to her arm.

They moved through the throng. Here in the District, the city of Kor Magna seemed so different. Everything was glossy, chic, and modern. Without the aliens, she could almost imagine she was standing in a casino in Las Vegas.

She stared at a group of beings sprawled in a cluster of chairs, blissed out expressions on their faces. A haze of smoke hung over them, and they were passing some sort of pipe between them. Laughter came from another group crowded around a table with a holographic game projected on it. And by the wall, two female aliens were kissing each other like no one else was in the room.

Lots of people stared at Regan. She knew she was different, an oddity, and she hated being the center of attention. She sucked in a breath. She was going to have to get used to that.

Galen led them to a bank of glass tubes that looked like elevators. Smooth curved doors slid open silently when they approached. They stepped inside, and when the doors closed, the capsule moved upward smoothly and silently.

"Are you okay?" Thorin pressed a hand to the small of her back.

She nodded, drawing in a deep breath. "I'm ready."

"We're heading to one of the top floors," Galen said. "Rillian has organized a private room for tonight's party."

"What's Rillian's full name?" Regan asked, mostly to keep her brain occupied.

"That's it, just Rillian," Galen responded. "No one knows if he has any others."

The lift slowed, and then the door slid open. They stepped into a hall that was painted matte black. Along it, she was surprised to see holographic, moving images of sleek women covered in gold paint, dancing.

A man stood before them, and she knew instantly he had to be the wealthy, mysterious Rillian.

He was outrageously good-looking, and wore a dark suit that fitted his body perfectly. Midnight-black hair brushed his shoulders, and his eyes were completely black as well. He was tall, but far leaner than the gladiators.

"Galen, welcome," the man said.

Galen nodded at the man. "Rillian, thanks for helping us out."

"I owed you." Rillian's gaze moved to Regan, and she saw his eyes change from black to a brilliant silver.

Regan blinked to make sure she hadn't imagined it. The man took her hand and bent over it, pressing his lips to her knuckles.

"You must be Regan." Rillian lifted his head. "Galen forgot to mention you were so petite and beautiful."

Thorin stepped closer, his chest touching her back. "Back off."

Rillian raised a dark brow. "Sorry. I didn't know she was taken. She is lovely. The Vorn will be in convulsions of joy when they see her."

Regan's stomach turned over, and she felt Thorin tense.

She cleared her throat. "We should get to the party." The sooner they did this, the sooner she'd be safely back at the House of Galen with Rory.

Rillian nodded, his silver eyes flashing. "Good luck."

They stepped inside a lovely, large room. Regan swallowed a gasp. The room was ringed by glass, and offered a brilliant view of Kor Magna.

The city stretched ahead. She saw the gambling strip of the District directly below, with its lights and fountains. Beyond that was the arena and the city. It was amazing to have a birds-eye view of the mammoth structure's ancient stone. And beyond the city, she saw desert stretching to the horizon, where the first of Carthago's suns was sinking past the edge of the planet.

She managed to rip her gaze off the view and focus on the room.

It was quite a classy party. A multitude of people stood around, dressed in glossy clothes, sipping foamy, multicolored drinks from long, slender glasses.

Galen leaned in close, his voice low. "The one standing across the room, examining the art piece on the wall...that's one of the Vorn."

Regan's hands went cold. The Vorn were tall, with lean hips, and a thick ridge running from their nose, up their forehead, and disappearing into their thick, curly hair.

Thorin reached around her and grabbed her hand. "You'll be fine."

She nodded. "I know."

Galen stepped forward. "We need to do a round. Show you off."

When the imperator held out his arm, she slid her arm through his. She shared one look with Thorin, saw so much moving through his gaze, and then they were walking.

Galen surprised her by having very refined manners. He stopped and chatted with various people, nodding and saying hellos.

She glanced up at him. He wore a shiny black eye patch tonight, and looked almost dashing.

He saw her looking at him. "What is it?"

"You. You're…charming."

He raised a brow. "I was raised to serve royalty, Regan. I wasn't only trained in battle."

Maybe not, but she could see that was in his blood. He'd saved his prince and then forged his house here to provide for them both. But she sensed such loneliness from him. That was something her captivity had trained her to recognize. She suspected it would take a very strong woman to break through Galen's shell.

Thorin stayed right behind them. Every time Regan looked up, she saw him watching her.

Then she scanned the room and saw the Imperator of the Vorn watching her.

She fought not to react. There was a crazed, hungry look in his eye—not lust, or at least, not a sexual lust. Just an avaricious need to possess.

Thorin made a low growling sound, and she turned away. They walked through the crowd some more. Regan didn't talk to anyone. She kept her eyes downcast, as people complimented Galen on her looks. Everything from her tiny size, to her smooth skin, to her golden hair. Her stomach churned.

Finally, they stopped near the window. Darkness had fallen, and Kor Magna was a sea of twinkling lights. If she'd expected a reprieve, however, she was sorely mistaken.

"Galen."

Her head jerked up. The Vorn imperator stood right behind her.

"Kuhl." Galen's voice didn't sound very friendly.

"She is as lovely as you said." Kuhl lifted a hand to touch her hair.

Thorin's hand snapped out and grabbed the imperator's wrist. The Vorn's expression turned outraged.

Galen swirled his drink. "She's not yours to touch, Kuhl."

"Yet," Kuhl snapped, yanking his hand back. Then the man pulled in a deep breath, his temper hidden. "Let's get a drink and talk." His gaze ran over Regan, like she was a piece of artwork. "I want her. Let's discuss what it's going to cost me."

"It's going to cost you extra, since you attacked one of my men and tried to abduct her from the market," Galen said dryly.

Regan wondered if anyone heard the cutting lethalness beneath those words. Man, she did not ever want to be on Galen's bad side.

Kuhl sipped his drink and shot Galen a wide grin. "I don't know what you're talking about."

But Regan saw in his eyes that he did. He knew, and he was responsible.

"You can bid on her at the auction," Galen said.

The imperator lifted a shoulder. "There's no need for an auction. I'll make you an offer that you won't be able to refuse. She will go very nicely with my feisty redheaded pet."

Regan's heart skipped a beat. There it was. Definitive proof that this man was holding Rory captive.

Galen stared hard at the man before he nodded. "Come."

The men settled into large comfy chairs off to the side of the room, right near the windows. A stunning female server with blue skin arrived, bringing drinks. Galen caught Regan's eye, and gestured for her to sit on the floor by his feet. She kneeled gracefully.

Thorin stepped close enough that his boots brushed her legs. That small touch steadied her.

The two imperators lifted their drinks, and got started with some small talk. Kuhl started describing one of the recent fights in the arena, as he pulled out a card and a writing instrument. He scribbled something on the card and tossed it at Galen, who caught it in a single move.

"That's what I'll pay for her." Kuhl sat back in his chair.

Galen glanced at the card, then lifted his glass. He swirled the ice and the bright-blue fluid in it. "Not enough. As far as we know, the Thraxians only nabbed a few humans of Earth before the transient wormhole they used to get to that system collapsed. They're rare."

Kuhl's eyes narrowed. "Rare, yes. But I heard the Thraxians got more than a few."

Regan's head snapped up. Kuhl shot her a smile that set her on edge. Thorin's leg moved against her, and she fought the urge to lean against him.

Kuhl tossed out a higher price.

Galen shook his head. "Double it."

Kuhl's jaw worked. Finally, he nodded. "Fine.

That's my last offer."

Galen was quiet for a moment. But she felt his focus on her, and Thorin's, and she knew Raiden was also nearby.

Then Galen nodded. "Sold."

Regan felt dizzy for a second. This was nothing like being violently grabbed by the Thraxians. She'd volunteered for this. She knew it wasn't real.

Kuhl grinned like a crazy man, and clapped his hands together.

She pressed her hands into her lap, and fought back a wave of nausea. This was what she'd wanted, to help Rory. But too many nightmares of her time with the Thraxians pushed their way to the surface. She kept her gaze on the floor.

Thorin's hand curled around her shoulder and squeezed. She realized she could feel a horrible tension throbbing off him.

"I think it's time I take my new acquisition away from the glare of your giant gladiator." Kuhl's gaze dropped to Thorin's hand. "And away from his rough hands. Something tells me he thinks the little woman is his."

Thorin made a deep growling sound.

"Thorin," Galen said, a warning.

"Come…pet." The Vorn imperator stood and held out a hand to her.

Regan hesitated. Then she reminded herself this was for Rory. Reluctantly, Regan reached out and put her hand in his.

He pulled her to her feet. "We're leaving."

She glanced briefly at Thorin, could see the

banked fury on his face. She saw Raiden step up close to his friend's side.

Then Kuhl pulled her away, and the crowd swallowed them. She was heading away from Thorin, from the safety of the House of Galen.

"You'll look so pretty in my collection." He leaned close, sniffing her. "And you smell pretty, too."

The guy was more than a little cracked. *Tracker.* She surreptitiously rubbed her wrist. She had the tracker. Now, she just had to find Rory, and disable the House of Vorn's security, and wait for her gladiators to come for her.

Thorin would come for her. *Don't take too long, Thorin.*

***

Thorin paced back and forth. He was going out of his mind. Letting Regan go with that crud-spawn...

"Take it easy, Thorin." Raiden squeezed Thorin's shoulder.

They stood in a private area of Rillian's suite, overlooking the casino. Thorin decided he hated the place: there was too much of everything. Too many people, too much tech, too much noise, and too much light.

Part of the charm of Kor Magna was that the arena hadn't changed much in hundreds of years. There was a sense of history in the stone, and on the sand of the arena floor. But it was more than that. It was a sense of stripping away all the tech and the trappings. It was man pitted against man in the most basic fashion.

But now, Regan was pitted against a far more dangerous opponent, and she'd gone with him armed with nothing but her wits.

"Okay, they're at the House of Vorn." Galen held up a small, hand-held screen he was staring at. Thorin could see a small, glowing dot that he knew represented Regan.

"You under control?" Raiden asked.

Thorin nodded. Regan needed him to keep his cool.

Rillian appeared, moving with the grace of a hunting cat. The man was all sleek charm and suave looks, but something about him set Thorin's senses off. He was dangerous, he just knew how to hide it.

The casino owner clasped his hands at the small of his back. "I do dislike the Vorn. They call themselves collectors, but they're crude. And crazy."

And they had Regan. Thorin growled.

"Our thanks for your help," Galen said.

The man nodded. "She's a nice girl." His gaze moved to Thorin. His eyes were black again, but now with shifting filaments of silver. "She's also a brave one. If there is anything more I can do to help, let me know." He looked back at Galen. "No marker required."

"We'll take it from here," Thorin said between gritted teeth.

Rillian nodded. "Good luck getting your woman."

Galen nodded and watched Rillian walk away, the light from the screen reflecting on his face. "Okay, let's get prepped and into position. Kace, Saff, and the others are waiting for us back at the House of Galen. Once Regan disables the security, we need to be ready to move."

On the return trip to the House of Galen, Thorin kept himself focused on the task. Back in his room, he stripped off his fancy clothes. He pulled on the all-black leathers they wore for their covert missions. He picked up his axe, sliding it into the strap on his back.

In the living area, he met the others. Raiden, Harper, Kace, and Saff were all dressed in black, like him. Small half masks hung around their necks. Carthago didn't have many laws, and beyond the city boundaries, there were none. But there were a few unwritten ones in the arena, and invading another house was always considered a breach worthy of retaliation. It was best they weren't identified, if things went wrong.

Nero and Lore entered. Nero was scowling. "I want in on this mission."

Raiden shook his head. "This is a simple extraction. We don't want to announce our presence."

"If you need help, just let us know," Lore added.

Galen arrived, also dressed in black. His sword hung from his hip.

"Security down?" Thorin asked.

Galen checked the screen strapped to his wrist. He shook his head.

Damn. What was taking her so long? Was she okay?

If Kuhl had hurt her...

Thorin felt his fury under his skin like a molten river. He felt scales flicker along his arm.

"Give it time," Raiden said. "She's smart."

Thorin shifted his feet. He knew that. But he hated waiting, wondering what was happening to her.

"Let's get into position," Galen said.

Soon, the six of them stepped into the tunnels, heading toward the House of Vorn. No one spoke, and they swiftly reached the House's entrance. The doors were flanked by guards, and the wood was engraved with a flowering vine motif.

Thorin and the others waited, their backs pressed against the stone. Galen checked the screen. Shook his head.

Come on, Regan. Thorin fought the urge to rush at the guards, tear them apart, and charge inside.

Then, he heard an almost inaudible beep. Galen looked up, a satisfied half smile on his face. "She did it." He nodded at them, and, as a group, they silently moved forward.

The guards lifted their heads at their appearance, but Thorin was on them before they could react. He took one down with a hard punch to the face, and was already spinning to meet the second one. Thorin gripped the stocky woman by her wrists, forcing her to drop her sword.

Sloppy. They were so used to knowing there was a high-tech security system in place, that they'd become complacent. A second later, both guards were slumped unconscious against the wall.

"Could have saved something for the rest of us," Saff grumbled under her breath.

Galen moved to the doors and pulled out a small device. He pressed the device to the large lock and tapped in a code. Lights blinked as the lock-breaker set to work. A tense moment passed, then the breaker beeped and the doors swung open.

They were in.

Galen turned to them in the faint light of the nearby lanterns. "Saff, Harper, you stay here on guard. No one comes in or out."

"What?" Saff looked like she wanted to argue. The woman always preferred to be in the thick of a fight, but Kace and Raiden had taken watch on the last mission.

Galen raised a brow, and Saff hissed out a breath. "You got it, G."

The four men stepped inside and paused.

"Hell," Raiden murmured.

There were plants everywhere. The lush, green smell hit Thorin in the face, overpowering his senses. The plants grew along the walls and up across the ceiling in a wild, tangled mess. Some were covered in flowers, some with giant thorns, and some had huge leaves as broad as Thorin's chest.

They lived amongst all this. Thorin shook his head. The Vorn were so weird.

"No guards?" Kace said quietly.

"They depend on the security system," Raiden said.

"No one's ever taken it down." Galen bent over his screen. "Kuhl must be too cheap to waste extra resources on guards. Regan's down on a lower level."

They crept through the plants, and Thorin spotted a corridor leading off to the side. He nodded his head to Raiden. They peered inside, and through the gloom, he saw living quarters, and heard the sound of voices talking, and plates rattling. It had to be where the Vorn kept their gladiators.

"Here," Kace whispered from somewhere close by.

Thorin and Raiden pushed through the foliage. Kace and Galen were standing beside a set of stairs that spiraled downward.

Together, they moved down the stone steps. The darkness grew, but near the bottom, Thorin could see a strange green glow ahead.

They stepped out of the stairwell and into another large room. Again, there were more plants everywhere, and some of them glowed a bright fluorescent green.

Thorin saw something move through the gloom, some sort of animal slinking between the plants. Overhead, birds started squawking.

Drak. The birds were going to give them away. The entire place reminded him of the hothouses the wealthy families had kept on his homeworld.

They moved into the wall of green, pushing

through the vegetation, and moving in the direction of Regan's location.

And then he spotted something else ahead, glimmering through the trees.

"Raiden," he murmured.

This time the glow was blue. Thorin pushed back a giant leaf and saw a row of energy cages.

As they got closer, he could see animals prowling behind the bars. Some were big cats with striped pelts and sharp fangs. Others were giant reptiles, with large horns and spikes along their backs. There were also a few humanoid aliens of different shapes and sizes.

He moved quietly along the row, his team behind him. The next cage held a long-limbed, blue-skinned woman, lounging on furs with a bored gaze. The final cage held an entire flock of tiny winged creatures.

Thorin's jaw locked. He hated the slaver Thraxians, but he decided he hated the Vorn just as much. At least the Thraxians were in-your-face about being crud-spawn slavers. The Vorn tried to pretty it up and pretend they were doing something good and interesting.

"Let's keep moving," Galen said.

They moved back into the dense foliage, moving in on Regan's location.

All of a sudden, the birds stopped squawking. Silence fell on them like a stifling blanket.

Thorin paused, arching his head up to stare at the overgrown branches and leaves overhead.

"I don't like this," Raiden muttered.

A large body dropped from the tree above and slammed into Thorin. He fell to his knees, and managed to grab the animal's powerful jaws before it locked them around his throat.

Dimly, he was aware of more creatures dropping from the trees onto the others.

Thorin found himself face-to-face with a creature he'd never seen before. It had jaws like a hunting cat, a single eye that glowed a burning gold, scales like a reptile, and dozens of strong tentacles that were wrapping around his arms and squeezing tight.

Drak. He caught sight of Raiden wrestling another creature on the ground, Kace standing with one clamped around his arms, and Galen slashing at a fourth creature with his sword.

Thorin swung around and slammed the creature into the trunk of a tree. It let out a screeching sound, the tentacles loosening a little.

Thorin managed to yank one hand free, grab his dagger off his thigh, and then slam it into the alien's eye.

It released him instantly and fell on the ground, flopping around, its tentacles writhing.

Then he reached back and pulled out his axe. He brought it down, severing the creature's head from its body. Then he strode over to help his friends.

As they all pulled free of the creatures, they heard growling from the trees ahead.

Shadows moved. Big ones.

"Ready?" he asked.

He heard swords being drawn, and saw the

swing of Kace's staff in the green glow.

"Ready," Raiden replied.

Giant canines loped out of the trees.

Thorin swung his axe, relieving one animal of its head. His fellow gladiators tore into the rest of the pack. Thorin slapped his axe handle against his palm. He saw some of the canines in back pause. They sniffed, scenting the blood of their comrades. They pulled back, growling in their throats. Then they disappeared into the vegetation.

Kace, Galen, and Raiden all flanked Thorin.

"Nice place," Raiden said, his tone dry. "I wonder what else the Vorn are hiding in their *collection*."

Yeah, well, Thorin didn't really want to find out. All he wanted was Regan back in his arms, and her cousin safe.

Moving forward, they found a path snaking through the greenery. Galen nodded, and they followed it until they reached an arched gateway made of worked metal.

"What now?" Raiden grumbled.

"We need to pass through this," Galen said. "Regan's on the other side."

Thorin pushed open the metal gate, and it swung wide with a metallic squeal. He stepped into what looked like some sort of giant cage, the top of it arching up to the roof.

Suddenly, a wild screech sounded above them.

"Aw, drak," Thorin spat out. They raised their weapons.

Raiden and Galen's swords glinted in the light given off by the plants. Kace spun his staff, getting a better grip, and Thorin hefted his axe.

Something swooped down from above. Thorin heard the flap of wings echoing in the space around them. There was another screech, and an entire flock of birds with giant claws dived at them.

Thorin swung his axe above his head, catching one bird and sending it flying. There were grunts and curses as the others fought. Thorin kept swinging, but one got past him, its claws tearing at the skin at the back of his neck. With a roar, he spun, and slammed his weapon into another vicious bird.

Finally, all the birds were down. Thorin rested his axe head on the ground, sucking in air. He glanced at the others. Raiden and Kace had scratches across their chests, their skin visible through the tears in their black shirts. Galen's cheek was split open, blood dripping down his face.

"Let's get Regan and her cousin and get the hell out of here," Raiden suggested. "I'm not planning to come back for a visit anytime soon."

They shoved their way out of the aviary, following the path through some more trees, when suddenly, the greenery thinned out into a clearing. Thorin still couldn't believe that the Vorn had built this place beneath the arena. This immense space, filled with jungle plants and animals that should be free.

Galen moved ahead. "Not far now. She should be—"

A giant net shot out from somewhere, tangling around Galen's body. The force of it knocked the imperator off his feet, and slammed him into a nearby tree. The net ropes moved, twining together and holding him fast. With a roar, Galen shoved against the ropes.

Raiden and Kace rushed to help him. As soon as they stepped off the path, the ground disappeared beneath them.

"No!" Thorin yelled.

Both men fell into huge holes in the floor.

"Raiden? Kace?" Thorin peered down into the blackness.

"I'm okay," Raiden called out.

"Me too," Kace replied.

Thorin looked at Galen. The imperator's eye patch was askew, but in the darkness, Thorin couldn't see what lay beneath it. As far as he knew, no one in the House of Galen knew how their imperator had lost his eye.

Galen looked pissed, his jaw locked, but he wasn't injured.

Thorin stood at the edge of the path, weighing his options. He was torn between helping his friends and saving his woman.

Then Raiden shouted, "Go find her, Thorin. We'll find a way out of here."

Then he heard Kace cursing—the man rarely cursed—and some deep animal snarls coming from the pit.

"Go, Thorin," Galen ordered.

With a single nod, Thorin hefted his axe and moved back down the path. Yep, it was official, he hated the Vorn.

The green bioluminescence from the plants slowly disappeared, leaving him in complete darkness. His steps slowed and he reached out with his senses. The gravel crunched loudly under his boots, and the only thing he could smell was flowers.

Suddenly, a light clicked on, blinding him.

Thorin held a hand up and ahead, a blur resolved itself into Kuhl.

The imperator was sitting on a large chair made of twisted trees, like it was a damn jungle throne. Behind him was an impressive display of alien weapons—daggers, poisoned sticks, firearms. They sat on a carved shelf designed to show them off. He was stroking a small winged animal in his arms. The creature looked up at Thorin and blinked its huge dark eyes. Then it hissed and bared pointed teeth.

Then Thorin heard a small gasp. He turned his head and spotted Regan.

She was standing by Kuhl's chair. She wasn't in her party dress anymore, but instead, wore a short skirt, and a small twist of metal covering her breasts. A thick chain lay around her neck, the back of it leading up to where the Vorn sat.

And beside Regan, wearing a similar outfit, with her hands cuffed together, was a clearly exhausted—but defiant looking—woman with red hair.

Chapter Fourteen

Thorin was here.

The thought reverberated in Regan's head, her pulse racing. She'd heard the fighting and endured Kuhl's glee as he'd informed her that Galen and his men had been trapped.

But clearly, Thorin hadn't.

Regan forced her fear down. She knew Rory was hurt, her face bruised. In the short time Regan had been here, all she'd heard was Rory snapping smartass comments at the Vorn imperator.

The man might consider Rory a pet, but he didn't mind hitting her.

"It'll be okay," she whispered quietly to her cousin.

Rory looked away. "Your friends aren't doing so well right now."

"You don't know them like I do. They're fierce fighters. And Thorin…" She looked at him now, standing tall and powerful. "He never gives up."

There was anger in his face, and the way his hands clutched the handle of his axe told her he was beyond control. She knew that under his black shirt, his scales would be showing.

"You have invaded my domain," Kuhl said.

"That means I can defend it with lethal force."

"You can try," Thorin said.

Kuhl lifted a hand and Vorn guards rushed in from all sides.

With a roar, Thorin swung his axe in a circle. He fought with brutal blows, giving no quarter. The sound of the fight rang in Regan's ears.

"You shouldn't have come, Regan," Rory muttered.

"Like I'd leave you here!"

"You should have stayed safe!"

Regan ignored her cousin, and slid her hands down to her ankles. She brushed her skin until she found the small, thin adhesives that Lore had given her. She looked up to make sure Kuhl was still occupied, then peeled one off and handed one over to her cousin. "These are tiny explosives. Put this on your cuffs; it'll melt through."

Rory took it. "It won't blow my hands off?"

"I hope not."

Rory shot her a look then bent over her cuffs. Quickly, Regan pressed the second adhesive to her own cuffs.

A pained roar echoed around them. Regan turned. *No!*

Three guards had attacked Thorin at once, with long stun weapons that glowed blue at the ends. He was down on his hands and knees, his axe gone, struggling to get up. Another guard came behind, raising his stun weapon.

Heart pumping and her mind going blank, Regan lurched forward.

"Uh-uh." The chain around her neck was jerked and she was yanked backward. "I knew this brute wanted you for himself," Kuhl ground out.

She glared at him. "You're the brute, not him. You pretend you're cultured and enlightened, but you enslave people. You're barbaric. Thorin is a hundred times the man you'll ever be."

The imperator's gaze narrowed. "That beast better not have had you. Better not have slobbered all over my pet."

She smiled. "Oh, he's had me. Over and over again. And I loved every minute of it."

Kuhl jerked her chain violently, and she stumbled. He yanked her until she was pressed against his legs, his hand tangling in her hair.

"He is nothing but a fighter, a weapon. No better than an animal." Kuhl twisted her head painfully to watch the fight. "Look at him. He's fighting like a wild man."

Thorin did look wild. He'd managed to bring down two guards and steal a stun weapon. He swung it, tearing into the guards. He had a terrible look on his face.

But she knew the real Thorin. She knew the heart of him. "He's a good man. And I love him."

From beside her, Rory gasped. Kuhl smiled. It was a mean smile.

Regan felt her stomach turn over. Too late, she remembered the rule of the arena. *Don't show your hand. Don't let them know you care.* Well, she'd just shoved her feelings out there, spotlighted, for Kuhl and everyone to see.

Suddenly, she felt the adhesive burn through her cuffs, and they fell free. All the anger and fear for Rory, Thorin, herself, and the others coalesced inside her. She gripped her chain and leaped onto Kuhl. She threw the metal around his neck and yanked back on it, choking him.

The Vorn imperator grunted and struggled. Regan kept pulling, with all the strength she had, her muscles straining.

Suddenly, Kuhl swung out his arms and backhanded her viciously. The blow made her head ring. The chain slipped through her hands and she slammed to the floor.

Then Kuhl loomed over her. He grabbed her by the neck, and dragged her up. He pushed her neck to the side until she felt the muscles burning from the strain.

"One small twist and I can break your neck."

She saw Rory on her knees nearby, watching, with fear and determination lining her face. She was pulling herself into a crouch, tensed to attack.

"That's far enough, gladiator." Kuhl dragged her around and she saw Thorin moving toward them.

Thorin paused, air sawing in and out of his lungs. He took another step toward them, but Kuhl pushed her head another painful inch. She cried out.

"No," Kuhl warned. "One more step, and I will break her lovely neck."

***

Thorin tried to calm his rage and fury. As he stood there, he smelled the sharp scent of Regan's fear.

Kuhl would die for that.

The imperator shook his head. "A brute like you doesn't deserve a beauty like this." With his other hand he reached out and stroked Regan's golden hair.

"You don't know the first thing about her beauty," Thorin spat out. Kuhl knew nothing of her smart mind, her sweet curves, her dedication to her friends. The Vorn only saw something shiny for his collection.

"Your big, rough hands shouldn't be allowed on her smooth skin," Kuhl said.

The words wormed through Thorin's skin, and stung. His hands flexed on his weapon.

"She's sweet, delicate," Kuhl continued. "You can't give her what she needs."

Regan jerked against the man's hold. He shook her, never letting up on the terrible angle he was holding her head at.

Thorin ground his teeth together, fighting the urge to lunge forward and strike the man down. He had to think. Behind him, he could scent more guards creeping forward to surround him. It was all just a ploy by Kuhl to let his fighters move into position.

"You have no idea what she needs," Thorin said.

Kuhl stroked Regan's cheek. "And you do? A big, vicious killer?"

Thorin stayed silent.

"She needs care. And love." The imperator

smiled at Thorin, then leaned over and licked Regan's cheek.

She flinched, but kept her gaze steady on Thorin.

"Has he told you that he loves you, little sweet Earth girl?" Kuhl said.

Her lips trembled. "No."

"And you know of all the women he fucks right after each fight? Sometimes up against the wall in the tunnels."

Her eyes flickered. "Yes."

"And still you love him?"

Thorin's body jerked. She loved him?

Her gaze touched his. "Yes."

Something inside his chest broke free, soaring. Regan loved him. He forced himself not to react to that startling news. If he gave anything away, Kuhl wouldn't hesitate to use it against him. Against Regan.

"Well, gladiator? Do you love her?"

"Are you playing matchmaker, Kuhl?" Thorin snapped out.

"Proving a point. Answer me or you'll hear her bones break."

Drak. Thorin couldn't admit what he felt. Hell, he knew nothing of love, and he wasn't exactly sure what this mix of hot emotion inside him was. All he knew was that was right now, he had to do what was necessary to save her.

"No," Thorin said.

"No, what, gladiator?"

Son of a crud-spawn. "No, I don't love her."

He saw Regan flinch. He wanted to roar. He wanted to smack his fist into Kuhl's face.

The imperator looked smug and lifted a hand.

The guards from the shadows rushed forward in a large group.

Thorin knew there were too many. Even as he turned and fought them, he knew he'd be overpowered. He still fought, swinging his stolen stunner. Bones cracked, guards groaned and some screamed in pain.

The image of Regan's shattered face fueled him. He fought until he was covered in blood, his hands slippery on the weapon.

Then a body rushed past him, knocking into a guard. Light glinted off a sword.

Raiden, Galen, and Kace joined the fight. With a battle cry, Thorin turned and fought beside his best friend. For a second, he was sure they were going to win.

"Kill them!" Kuhl yelled. "I want them dead."

Thorin heard a low-pitched whistle and saw more guards coming, along with various dangerous animals that were slinking out of the vegetation. He saw a giant canine moving forward, drool dropping from its fangs.

There were too many.

Thorin's chest constricted. He looked at Regan, still held in Kuhl's grip.

A spasm ran through Thorin, something deep inside clawing at his chest. He was the only person that could save Regan now.

And in order to do that, he would have to let his

dark side loose.

Regan might think she loved him—but once she'd seen what was really inside him, what people truly feared, she'd change her mind.

But he'd risk that to save his woman.

Thorin let out a roar. All conscious thought fell away, and he felt a ripple over his skin. His muscles burst free, shredding his shirt, his dark scales covering every inch of his skin.

His next roar sounded more guttural, and his senses exploded outward.

He dropped his weapon and lifted hands tipped by claws. He sniffed, scenting friend and foe. And another, more delicate, fragrance.

Mate. Protect mate.

He tore into his attackers.

***

Regan watched Thorin...transform.

He still stood on two feet, but the dark scales covered his entire body now, a long tail kept him balanced, and dark, leathery wings had sprung from his back. He ripped into the Vorn guards with giant clawed hands, moving faster than she'd seen anyone move before.

He looked like...a humanoid dragon.

Bodies flew through the air, screams echoing around them.

Raiden, Galen, and Kace had pulled back, all of them watching Thorin with a heavy intensity. They all kept their weapons up.

This was what Thorin had hinted at. This was the demon he'd kept hidden.

This was what he was so afraid of.

"Regan?" Rory's whisper.

Her cousin moved closer, and Regan noticed that her hands were free. Regan tried not to look down and let Kuhl—who was watching Thorin in a shocked stupor—realize Rory was close. She blinked at her cousin.

Rory gestured at Kuhl. Regan considered. Together, the two of them might have a chance of taking the imperator down. Kuhl was watching the fight, slack-jawed, something moving through his eyes.

He wasn't nervous. No, she saw that same desire that she'd seen when he'd looked at her at the party.

He was imagining Thorin caged. A wild, exotic beast for Kuhl's viewing pleasure.

No way. Thorin didn't love her. His blank face as Kuhl had forced the confession from him had almost killed her. But so what? No one had ever loved her. She still loved him, and wasn't going to let him be captured or killed.

She caught Rory's gaze again, and her cousin nodded.

As Rory reared up, Regan spun. Together, they attacked the man. As both their bodies hit him, he went over backward.

But he recovered his balance quickly and didn't go down. He stumbled, swinging at them. Rory jumped and landed on his back. She yanked his arms back. Regan kicked him, catching him in the thigh. Rory and Kuhl went down in a tangle of arms and legs.

Regan heaved in a breath and watched as Rory wrestled the bigger man, pinning him and bending his arm back at an unnatural angle. She knew her cousin was trained in mixed-martial arts, and this time she wasn't sticking to any rules. Kuhl's face showed shock at the fierceness of Rory's fighting.

Regan turned her head and spotted the row of weapons lined up behind Kuhl's ugly-ass throne. She raced over, her gaze locked on a jeweled dagger.

She snatched it off the stand.

Suddenly, Kuhl let out an angry shout. There was the horrible sound of bone on flesh, and Regan winced. She spun and saw Rory falling back with a cry.

Regan leaped forward with the dagger. Kuhl blocked her, his arm slamming against hers. Pain rocketed through her arm.

He swung at her again and she spun, ducking the hit. She remembered the few moves that Thorin had taught her, and stabbed the dagger at Kuhl.

He dodged. "You can't beat me, little thing."

She was so sick of everyone calling her little. She jumped up and stabbed again.

He screamed and Regan gasped, blood splattering her.

She'd embedded the dagger in his eye.

Kuhl staggered back, a hand pressed to his

bleeding eye. He fell to his knees, still screaming. Then he collapsed, curling into a ball.

"Are you both okay?"

Regan looked up, raising her hands to protect herself.

Galen watched her steadily, holding his hands up, a sword clasped in one.

Her shoulders relaxed. "We're okay." She moved over to Rory, sliding her arm around her cousin's shoulders. "We're fine."

Galen knelt and gestured to the chains still attached to their necks. It only took him seconds to get them off.

Regan breathed a sigh of relief.

Rory leaned into her. Her face was turning purple from Kuhl's hit. "We're fine, but I'm not sure he is, though." She nodded her head.

They all turned.

Regan's muscles locked. *Thorin.*

He was standing amid a pile of groaning, bleeding bodies. He was covered in blood and gore, air whistling in and out of his lungs.

Kace and Raiden stood nearby. They'd both lost their shirts and looked pretty battered. Raiden had scratches across his chest, and one of Kace's eyes was swollen shut. But they were standing, tense and ready, staring at Thorin.

Thorin's chin pressed to his chest, and his hands clenched into giant fists, the muscles in his arms flexing.

In the next moment, his tail and wings were gone, although his scales were still visible, but

Regan could tell they were slowly fading.

And all of them were standing there, looking at him like he was some wild animal they had to be wary of.

Afraid of him, just like the cowardly family who'd dumped him here.

No. Regan stepped forward.

Rory grabbed her arm.

"It's okay," Regan said.

Rory didn't look convinced, but she released Regan's arm. She walked toward Thorin. He might look different, but he was still Thorin. Her Thorin.

He'd denied this part of himself for so long. Hidden it because he knew it was dangerous and scared people. She refused to be afraid of him.

She got closer. He didn't love her, but he felt something. He cared in his own way. And despite everything, she loved him. All of him.

She stopped in front of him.

He raised his head, his gaze burning as he looked at her. Then suddenly, his arm shot out and he grabbed her, yanking her to his chest. He pulled her up so her feet dangled off the ground.

She heard the others gasp.

Then he pressed his face into her neck, sniffing her.

She stroked his sweat-dampened hair. "I'm here Thorin. I'm here."

***

With Regan's sweet scent filling his nostrils, Thorin

183

slowly felt himself calming down. The beast that lived inside him was going back to sleep. *Regan. His mate*. His Regan.

She pulled back, looking up at him. "Thorin, are you all right?"

He nodded. "You...saw." His voice cracked.

"You were remarkable." She stroked her hand down his arm, over the last of the fading scales. "I want to know all about it. How the change happens. How it feels. Maybe I could take a sample of your blood and tissue, and look at your cells under the machine Galen's getting for me."

She peppered him with more questions. Of course, his little scientist was curious.

"You are not afraid?"

She blinked. "Of you? Why would I be?"

A tight knot inside of him unraveled. He reached up and touched her cheek.

And that's when he saw her eyes go cool. She pulled back, wiggling for him to let her down. He reluctantly let go of her.

"Thanks for coming for me," she said.

He tilted his head. Her voice was polite and cool.

Suddenly, a scream echoed around them. They spun and Thorin saw Kuhl on his feet, looking gruesome. He had yanked the dagger out of his eye, and had an arm wrapped around Rory. He was dragging her away from his throne and into the shadows.

Thorin pushed forward, his friends stepping up beside him. Kuhl pulled Rory through a gate and disappeared.

"Rory!" Regan cried out.

"We'll get her," Raiden said.

They all moved forward. Passing through the gate, they entered an overgrown garden covered in flowers. The bioluminescence was brighter here, and thick, green grass grew knee high.

They heard a cry ahead, and followed. Thorin pulled Regan closer to him.

As he took another step, something moved off to their left. The gladiators paused.

Something shot out of the darkness that looked like snakes.

"Vines!" Regan shouted.

"Thorin." Raiden threw Thorin a sword.

Together, they all swung their weapons, slashing through the fast-moving vegetation. But as quick as they cut them, more raced forward, like giant, possessed snakes.

One vine wrapped around Galen's body, dragging him down. He cursed, hacking at it with his sword.

"Keep going!" the imperator yelled at them.

Faces grim, they did, moving forward. A dense group of trees blocked their way. Raiden went first, lifting his sword.

The trees all bent down, attacking him, the whisper of leaves sounding like demonic voices. One of the branches wrapped around Raiden and lifted him up, shaking him. Thorin raced forward with a shout. He grabbed Raiden's ankle.

"Find Rory," Raiden called out. He swung his sword at the tree, working to cut himself loose.

Drak. Thorin saw Regan watching him with huge eyes. He looked at Kace, and the other man nodded. They pushed Regan tight between them. He wanted her to go back, but he also didn't want her out of his sight. Who knew what else Kuhl had in this house of horrors?

A horrid stench hit Thorin's senses. Ahead was a wall of beautiful pink flowers.

As Kace moved forward to push them apart, Thorin grabbed his arm. "Stop." He sniffed again.

"What's wrong?" Kace demanded.

"They smell bad."

"I don't smell anything."

Regan leaned closer, studying the blooms. "Bright blooms and they have some pink berries clustered at the base." She frowned. "All things designed to attract you to touch it." She looked up. "I think they might be poisonous."

A second after she spoke, the closest flowers opened up, unfurling like a gift. They let out a small puff of mist.

Thorin dragged Regan back.

"Don't breathe it in," she warned.

Kace nodded his head off to the right. "Look. There's a pathway heading that way."

The three of them moved cautiously toward the path that went in a smooth curve. Ahead, they could see that the path was lined by large plants with enormous, bright-yellow, bell-shaped flowers. They were as long as Kace and Thorin.

As they stalked past, one flower moved.

Thorin paused and lifted his sword.

Another flower moved, rising up high.

Then it shot down, like a striking snake, engulfing Regan.

"Regan!" Thorin shouted.

She struggled, and the smooth petals wrapped more tightly around her. Thorin ripped at the plant, tearing at the petals.

The yellow flower was tough and fibrous. He couldn't get it open. "Hold on, Regan."

She was twisting and jerking, her hands pressed against the flower.

Somewhere ahead of them, there was a loud scream.

Drak. "Kace, find the woman." Thorin felt his scales rising to the surface.

"On it. You take care of Regan."

Thorin didn't watch his friend leave. He used his sword and carefully split the flower open. Then he grabbed the ragged edges and tore them wider. Regan's terrified face appeared. Her body was still stuck fast in the flower.

"Heat. I have a plant like this back in the lab." Her nose wrinkled. "A smaller version. It dislikes heat."

Thorin pulled out his dagger. He grabbed a rock off the ground and struck his blade against it. A spark gleamed in the darkness. He did it again, holding it close to a pile of dry leaves on the ground. The leaves caught fire and he stepped backward.

The plants started shaking and let out a high-pitched screech.

The flower released Regan, shrinking back, and she stumbled toward Thorin. He caught her, pulling her in for a hug.

Then he looked up, just in time to see the plant attacking them again. A bell-shaped flower rushed toward them. Its petals opened up, and he could see a sharp, beak-like mouth inside.

Gritting his teeth, he turned, shielding Regan with his body. He felt a sharp sting as something slammed into his shoulder.

Regan muttered a curse he didn't recognize, grabbed his knife from his hand, then leaned back and reached behind him, stabbing at the flower, punctuating her words with sharp thrusts of the dagger.

"I have had a shitty day." Stab. Stab. "I do not need—" stab, stab "—a giant plant eating me!"

With another screech, the plant pulled away.

"Thanks." He looked over his shoulder at the spot where the flower had bitten him, and he grimaced at what looked like a large set of bloody teeth marks on his skin.

But he couldn't worry about that right now. He pressed a quick kiss to Regan's lips. "Let's go find your cousin."

Chapter Fifteen

Kace

Kace stared at the thick vegetation. As always, he let none of his distaste show on his face.

A perfect Antarian Military Commander never showed his true feelings. Rule Number 4 of the Antar Military Code of Conduct.

He pressed a button on his staff and knives slid out at both ends. He lifted it and started hacking through the thick greenery.

He was from a grassland world. He hated this thick, suffocating plant life. He pushed on, however, and soon, he stepped out into a small clearing.

Ahead, he saw the woman wrestling with Kuhl, rolling through the long grass. She was small, but she appeared to be strong and determined.

She managed to flip the injured Vorn onto his back, landing on his chest and pinning him down.

She was...incredible.

A rustling sound came from the grass off to his right. Vines shot out of the trees nearby.

No! They wrapped around the woman's wrists, holding her in place. She struggled, trying to get free. But the vines held her long enough for Kuhl to rear up. He landed a hard fist to her stomach, and Rory groaned.

Jaw tight, Kace sprinted forward.

Kuhl landed another punch, slamming his knuckles into her face, snapping her head back.

Kace felt a cold anger race through him. On Antar, it was considered cowardly to attack someone weaker than yourself. It was dishonorable to beat and abuse another living being.

He rushed in, using his staff to slice through the vines holding her. She looked up and he saw brilliant eyes of gold-flecked green.

Before he could stop her, or even say a word, the woman leaped up, spun, and slammed a kick into Kace's belly. It knocked the air out of him. Unprepared for her unexpected attack, Kace wheezed in air, just as her second kick brought him to his knees.

Dazed, he watched as she followed that by giving Kuhl a hard kick to the head.

"That's for being a grade-A asshole." She kicked the imperator again.

Kace moved, and like a wild woman, she turned to him. She dived, tackling Kace to the ground.

"No one is taking me prisoner again. Got it?"

They rolled across the grass and finally they ended with her flinging him onto his back. She landed on top of him and punched him in the face. *By the Creators.* Kace tried desperately to grab her without hurting her.

She gripped his arm, bending it so hard that

pain shot through him like a spear. Drak, she was vicious.

"I'm here to help you," he bit out.

She hesitated, staring into his eyes. Her unique red hair was tangled around her bruised face. He hated seeing what Kuhl had done to her.

Suddenly, movement over her shoulder caught his gaze. Kuhl was advancing on them.

"Watch out!" Kace called out.

She rolled off him, reached out, and grabbed his staff, then leaped to her feet. She spun to face the oncoming attack.

Kuhl swung his fist at her.

Kace pushed to his feet, ready to intervene. She jabbed awkwardly at Kuhl with Kace's staff, and instantly, he saw that she wasn't trained in staff fighting.

The Vorn grabbed the end of the staff, the built-in knife slicing his hand open, sending blood dripping down his fingers.

Crazy bastard. Kace moved forward slowly.

Rory and the imperator started a tug-of-war over the staff. But Rory couldn't match the Vorn for strength.

When Kuhl took possession of the staff and grinned, Kace had had enough.

As Kuhl swung the staff at her, Kace blocked the man's hit.

With that cold anger driving him, Kace yanked his staff from the man. He spun it, retracting the knives, and swung at Kuhl.

It smacked into the man's chest, sending him

staggering. Kace advanced, landing vicious blows. A hit to the chest, a hard hit to the arm, a knock into his side.

Kuhl let out pained grunts, swinging wildly, trying to fight back.

Kace landed a hard kick to Kuhl's gut and then brought the staff down on the back of the Vorn's neck. He dropped like a stone, blood dripping down his face.

He looked back at the woman. She was standing there watching him, that fierce look in her green-gold eyes. The bruises did nothing to diminish it.

"What now, pretty boy?" she asked.

Pretty boy? He raised a brow. Despite everything that had been done to her, this woman wasn't cowed or beaten. She had spirit.

Kace stepped back and extended his staff to her. She watched him intently. "Take it. Finish it. You've earned the right."

Her hands closed around the metal that Kace's hands knew intimately. He saw a shiver go through her, before she straightened.

She stepped forward and hit Kuhl hard in the head, knocking him out cold. Then she just stood there looking down at the Vorn imperator.

"You're not going to kill him?" Kace asked.

She pulled in a shuddering breath and handed the staff back to him. "I won't let him turn me into something I'm not. I'm not a killer."

Kace took his weapon, spinning it under his arm. She didn't just have spirit. These women of Earth had spines made of steel.

"I'm Kace. A friend of Regan and Harper."

Now the redhead's lips trembled. "I'm Rory and I'm looking forward to seeing my friend and cousin, and getting out of here. Thanks for the rescue, Kace." She looked at his face and winced. "Sorry, it looks like I gave you a black eye."

Both his eyes throbbed, and one was already swollen shut. "It'll match the other one." His gaze moved over the fascinating sprinkle of darker spots across her nose. "We need to find the others. They were all caught in the vegetation. I promised Regan I'd get you."

She wrapped her arms around her middle, showing the first sign of vulnerability he'd seen in her.

He took a step back in the direction he'd come.

"Kace?"

He looked back at her. "Yes?"

"My leg's broken."

He cursed. He hurried back to her. She'd fought like a warrior all this time with a broken leg? He scooped her up into his arms. "You women of Earth are so stubborn."

"And gladiators aren't?"

He strode down the path, shouldering through the vegetation, which, surprisingly, now let them pass without interference. She was a small, warm, and vital bundle against his chest. Her gaze was direct, strength in it.

Kace had always been attracted to strength.

He looked away. Women were not on his agenda. He was on Carthago for a reason, and his time here was finite. He had duties that demanded his loyalty and attention.

They didn't include a little redhead from Earth.

Suddenly, Regan and Thorin burst out of the bushes ahead.

"Rory!" Regan cried.

Kace's hands tightened briefly, then he handed Rory over to her cousin and Thorin. She had people to look after her. She wasn't Kace's responsibility. He had enough of those.

***

Showered and changed, Regan made her way down to Medical to check on Rory, all the while trying very, very hard not to think about Thorin.

He'd demanded they talk when they returned to the House of Galen, but like a 'fraidy cat, she'd held him off, saying she needed to clean up and rest.

She couldn't bear to hear him lay out all the reasons he didn't love her.

Just as she reached the doors to Medical, Kace pushed out of the room.

"How is she?" Regan asked.

"Healed," the gladiator said, his now-healed face unreadable. With a nod, he left.

As Regan entered the large, airy room, she saw that Rory was just being helped out of a regen tank by one of the tall, slender, and genderless Hermia healers.

Regan hurried over to her cousin and helped wrap her in a robe. "How do you feel?"

"Pretty darn good, considering." The bruises on Rory's face were gone, leaving only her natural scattering of freckles across her nose. Rory pulled Regan in for a hug. "Thanks to you. Thanks for getting me out."

Regan hugged her cousin tight. She could hardly believe Rory was finally safe. "Love you."

Rory made a noise that sounded an awful lot like a sniffle. Her tough cousin never cried. "You too." Rory pulled back. "Harper already visited me." A wide grin. "She's going to teach me some gladiator moves." Then Rory's smile disappeared. "She also told me we can't go home."

Regan grabbed Rory's hands, holding them tight. "No, we can't. I know it will take some time to accept and understand it. You okay with that?"

"Not really. You're right; I'll need some time to digest it all. My family..." Rory dragged in a deep breath.

Regan nodded. "I know. I wasn't close to mine like you were, but I still miss them."

"God, Regan...my parents, my brothers. They'll be devastated. It breaks my heart that they'll never know what happened. And I know your parents could be difficult—"

"You call them Mr. and Mrs. Asshole."

Rory sniffed. "Seems a bit mean, now. But they are judgmental, selfish people, Regan. They treated you like shit, but I still think they'd be sad."

Regan gave her cousin a rueful smile. "No, they wouldn't have been. Sad that I didn't marry the perfect man and pop out perfect grandkids. Sad that I didn't give up my silly career. But sad that I'm gone...I kind of think they would have been relieved."

Rory gripped Regan's shoulders. "It's their loss, Regan." A cheeky smile crossed her face. "I have to admit, I would've liked to see them lay eyes on your big gladiator."

Imagining her parents taking in Thorin made Regan burst out laughing. Then a slashing pain crossed her chest. She swallowed. "He's not mine. He...he doesn't love me. We were just having some fun. I think I'm just an interesting diversion for him for a little while."

Rory paused in belting her robe more tightly. "I don't know everyone here yet, and just between you and me, I am steering clear of scary Galen as much as I can. But from what I saw, Thorin fought for you. He literally turned into a beast to protect you."

"He's a good man, but I can't make him love me. I'm done trying to make people love me, Rory."

Rory's brow creased. "I don't know. I saw the way he looked at you—"

Suddenly, the door slammed open, and Raiden rushed in. "Healers, you're needed. Now."

Regan jumped, watching as the Hermia healers gathered their gear. "What's wrong?"

Raiden turned, his face face. "It's Thorin."

Regan's heart spasmed. "What's wrong with him?"

"We're not sure. He's sick."

As the healers raced out with Raiden, Regan and Rory rushed after them.

When they reached Thorin's room, she saw him lying on his bed, on his side, unmoving. His chest was bare, and the sheets were a perspiration-soaked tangle around his lower body.

His shoulder was an angry red, and swollen, where the plant had bitten him.

The healers knelt by the bed and set to work. Regan moved closer, circling around to the other side. Suddenly, Thorin began tossing and turning, sweat beading on his face.

Raiden put his arm around Harper, both of them watching Thorin with concern.

Screw this. "Thorin." Regan climbed onto the bed. She touched his forehead. God, he was so hot. Too hot.

"Here." One of the healers handed her a cloth.

She nodded and started to run it over his face. He turned toward her, his eyes glazed, like he didn't recognize anybody.

Regan made herself look at the terrible wound. "It's infected."

One of the Hermia healers was already standing beside the bed, scanning Thorin's body with a small, hand-held device. The healer frowned. "No. It's poison."

Soft curses echoed around the room.

"But you can get it out of him, right?" Raiden asked.

The Hermia frowned at the screen. "I'm not sure. This poison has been genetically enhanced." The healer looked at them solemnly. "I have no treatment."

"What about the regen tank?" Regan asked.

"It won't help. Unless we can find an antidote for this particular poison, we cannot help him."

Regan pressed her hand to his arm, her hands flexing on his skin. "No."

"Regan?" The word was a harsh croak.

"Thorin." She pressed her hand against his cheek. His skin was on fire.

Galen strode in, his gaze running over Thorin. "What's going on?"

"Poison," Raiden answered. "No cure."

"Drakking Vorn," Galen bit out. He turned to the healers. "I want you in Medical *now*. I want the team working on finding an antidote for this." With nods, the healers glided out of the room.

"Hurt," Thorin said. "Thirsty."

Regan reached to the bedside table and grabbed a glass of water. She held it up to his lips so he could take a sip. "You've been poisoned. That plant bite injected a toxin into you." She set the drink down, pushing his damp hair off his face. "You got hurt protecting me."

"I'll always...protect you. Until I stop breathing."

Regan was so focused on him that she was only dimly aware of the healers leaving the room.

"I know you don't love me, Thorin, but that doesn't change the fact that I love you. I can't lose you, you need to fight this. I love every tough inch of you."

His eyes seemed to clear a little, staring at her directly. "You love me?"

"Yes."

"Even after you saw my inner..."

"Every inch."

"Regan." His hand reached for her. "I told Kuhl I didn't love you, so he wouldn't use it against you."

She went still.

"I'm not entirely sure what love is. I've never really experienced it, at least, not as an adult. I sometimes wonder if my family ever loved me, or if I was always just a useful abomination to them."

"You are *not* an abomination."

A faint smile flickered on his lips. "Regan, everything I have inside me, it's all for you. I love you, so much it scares me."

She felt tears pricking her eyes. She leaned down and pressed her lips to his. "Oh, Thorin."

"I've never said those words to anyone," he whispered. "And...my other side considers you its mate. Its mate for life."

Mate? The idea was startling. No one had ever wanted her so much as to claim her for life.

Suddenly, he groaned. She pulled back and saw pain race across his face. His muscles locked and he thrashed on the bed.

Dammit, she had to do something to help him.

"You hold on, Thorin." She leaped off the bed and yanked open the door. "Raiden, please stay with Thorin. Harper, I need things from my lab. Now!"

She wasn't letting her gladiator die.

***

He was hurting. Everything hurt.

Thorin opened his eyes and realized the room was blurry. Everything was covered in a haze. He looked over and distantly noted Regan, hunched over a table pushed up close to his bed. *Regan*. His everything. His mate.

He saw lines of stress bracketing her mouth, and she was focused on mixing things in various glasses on her desk. She turned, tapping on a glowing screen.

He tried to say something, but he couldn't move his lips. Then, he drifted away, floating in the blackness of pain.

When he came to next, Regan was forcing something down his throat. Something foul-smelling and bad tasting.

"Come on, Thorin," she murmured. She moved and he felt her press something cool to his throbbing, burning shoulder.

"You'll kill me with that smell," he managed to gasp out.

"Thorin!" He felt a quick kiss on his cheek. "This is going to hurt. Bad. I'm so sorry. We need to draw the toxin out of your body. This is the fourth version I've tried." She pressed her head to his chest. "Don't leave me." Ragged words. "I need you."

No one had ever truly needed him before. As a weapon, yes. As a fighter, definitely. But not just him—Thorin, the man.

Fire ripped through him. It started at his shoulder, racing through his body. He heard Regan murmuring to him, but he couldn't make out her words. He thrashed his head and caught sight of Raiden and Kace holding him down on the bed.

As the pain swelled, Thorin let out a roar. He saw Regan's face, tears tracking down her cheeks.

Then the blackness took him again.

Finally, he surfaced again, clear, morning light spilling through the window.

He shifted a little, waiting for the pain to tear into him again. But there was nothing. He felt fine. Tired and weary, but there was no burning agony.

He glanced down at his shoulder and saw a faint red ring, but other than that, there was no sign of the bite mark.

Then he noted the slight weight pressed against his side. He glanced lower and saw Regan curled in an exhausted ball beside him. With love filling his chest, he reached down and stroked his fingers through her hair.

"She tried to stay awake, but she lost the battle a couple of hours ago."

The female voice made Thorin carefully turn his head. Rory was sitting in a chair beside the bed. She reached over and offered him a drink.

He nodded and carefully took a sip. "You look better."

She smiled. "That should be my line."

"I don't mean the bruises."

She shrugged one shoulder. "I am not going to let the fucking Thraxians or Vorn have the satisfaction of keeping me down." Her lips firmed. "I've lost my planet, my family, my life...I won't lose myself as well."

Then she looked at Regan. "I consider myself lucky. I have Regan and Harper, and they tell me that all the people here at the House of Galen aren't so bad."

"You have all of us, Rory. Not just Harper and Regan," Thorin added quietly.

A quicksilver smile. "They both said this is a good place to start over."

Thorin managed a nod, feeling tired.

"She worked herself to the bone to find a way to draw the toxin out of your body," Rory said. "She wouldn't give up on you. I don't know all the scientific details, but she worked with the healers, and used stuff from all those plants down in her lab until she was sure she could save you."

He stroked Regan's hair.

"She loves you," Rory said.

"I know." He felt such a sense of wonder at that.

Rory sighed. "I had this big, overprotective-cousin speech prepared. I was planning to tell you that you needed to wake up and tell her that you love her. But one look at your face, and I think you know that. I think you'll look after her."

"Every minute of every day," he said. "She's my heart."

Rory smiled. "That'll do."

"Thorin?" Regan's sleepy voice.

With a wink, Rory stood and left the room.

Thorin looked down at the woman in his arms. She reached up and touched his shoulder. "It looks good. Thank God."

"Thanks to you. You saved me."

She reached up and cupped his cheeks. "It was my magic botany powers, actually, but really, I think we saved each other."

"I love that smart mind of yours."

She smiled. "Oh, and what else?"

"Your gentle fierceness, and your sexy side."

Her gaze traced his face. "You do love me, don't you?"

How could she doubt that? He cursed the people who'd made her feel that way. "I'll spend every day proving my love to you." He moved, rolling her beneath him on the bed. He moved his hips, nudging her with his hardening cock.

She shook her head. "You're supposed to stay in bed—"

"I am in bed."

"Resting," she said with exaggerated patience. "The Hermia gave you some supplements to help replenish your energy, but you still have to rest."

He moved against her. "I think we can safely say I'm feeling better." He pressed his lips to the side of her neck, loving when she squirmed against him. "If you're nearby, I'm hard. Love you, my sweet Earth girl. My mate."

"I love you too, my big gladiator. Hold on to me and don't ever let go."

"Never." A promise etched on his heart.

I hope you enjoyed Thorin and Regan's story!

Galactic Gladiators continues with HERO, the story of clean-cut, military gladiator Kace, and outspoken Earth engineer Rory. Read on for a preview of the first chapter.

Don't miss out! For updates about new releases, action romance info, free books, and other fun stuff, sign up for my VIP mailing list and get your *free box set* containing three action-packed romances.

Visit here to get started:

www.annahackettbooks.com

FREE BOX SET DOWNLOAD

JOIN THE ACTION-PACKED ADVENTURE!

Formats: Kindle, ePub, PDF

Preview: Hero

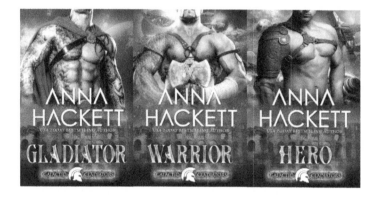

The sound echoed off the stone walls around him.

It wasn't thunder, or the roar of an engine. It was the combination of thousands of voices chanting his name.

Kace Tameron stood at the tunnel entrance and assimilated all the information. The heat of the setting suns on his skin. The thunder of the crowd sitting in the seats circling the arena. The bright strobe lights shining into the darkening sky.

His heartbeat stayed steady and he shifted his combat staff, the smooth steel cool and familiar against his palms. In his head, he ran through an Antarian fight chant to focus his thoughts.

Once he got the order, he'd step out onto the sand of the Kor Magna Arena.

It was the fiercest gladiatorial arena on the galaxy's outer rim. Where slaves fought for freedom, where fighters battled for glory, and where soldiers, like himself, came to hone their skills.

Around him, his fellow gladiators were stretching, checking their weapons, focusing their thoughts.

"I'm ready to smack some Thraxians into the sand," Thorin shouted, slapping the head of his axe against his palm.

Kace eyed the giant Sirrush gladiator. Thorin was a little wild and deadly on the sand. His fighting partner stood beside him, the champion of the Kor Magna Arena, Raiden Tiago. The man's tattoos gleamed on his bronze skin, and there was no missing the fact that he was built like a fighter, and not the prince he'd once been.

Just beyond them in the tunnel stood another fighting pair from the House of Galen. Mountainous Nero and showman Lore. Kace was a career soldier. He'd worked with some of the best fighters on his planet, but this team was beyond good.

Here, projectile weapons were banned and considered dishonorable. Here, most technology was frowned upon, too. Here, you fought up close and personal, and you had to be good.

It was one of the cardinal rules of the arena— and there weren't many rules in Kor Magna—that a gladiator not be enhanced, or controlled by tech. They fought robots, used some energy shields and weapons, and raced chariots. But at the end of the day, it was gladiator against gladiator, man against man.

Someone bumped his shoulder, and Kace looked down at his own fighting partner. Saff Essikani was grinning at him, her teeth white against her darker skin. Her long, black hair fell to her waist in a mass of tiny braids. She was tall and muscular, and a hell of a gladiator in the arena.

While eagerness wafted off Saff, Kace stayed still and composed.

He wasn't an arena slave fighting for freedom, or a lifer like his friends, who considered the desert world of Carthago and the city of Kor Magna home. Kace was military. Born and bred to fight. He was here on a contract for two years to hone his skills.

A man stepped in front of them, wearing all black. His black shirt covered one arm and left his other muscled bicep bare. He moved his powerful body with a precision that let you know he could burst into action when required. Kace recognized a fellow warrior when he saw one.

With a scarred face and a black eye patch over one eye, Galen, Imperator of the House of Galen, was an imposing man.

"I don't need to tell any of you to fight well. You do every time you step in the arena." His single icy-blue eye took them all in. "I will tell you that the House of Thrax is still very unhappy with us."

Kace knew that was an understatement. They'd

rescued several women from the Thraxians, and beaten the aliens time and again. Kace felt a very un-soldier-like lick of satisfaction. The Thraxians were slavers, and they deserved everything they got. They snatched people from all over the galaxy to sell to the highest bidders, and they'd made the unfortunate mistake of taking a transient wormhole to a distant star system on the opposite side of the galaxy.

They'd abducted a group of women off a space station near a planet called Earth. The diminutive women had also proven to be very tough and fierce. Thinking of them almost made him smile. The Thraxians hadn't known what hit them.

Kace, along with the other gladiators in the House of Galen, had helped free the Earth women. And now Harper, Regan, and Rory were stranded here, unable to return to their planet.

"The House of Thrax is looking for revenge," Galen said, his voice deep. "Watch yourselves out there."

Kace tightened his grip on his staff. It was of typical Antarian design—his people made some of the best weapons in the known galaxy. In the military, he also used ranged weapons, but here in the arena, it was considered cowardly. His proficiency with the staff had increased substantially in the six months he'd been a member of the House of Galen.

Right now, he was ready to pit himself against the Thraxian gladiators.

He heard footsteps behind them. He turned his

head and he saw Harper, one of the women of Earth, move forward. Her smile was centered on Raiden.

"We came to wish you luck," Harper said.

The tough gladiator snatched the woman up with one arm, and pulled her in for a kiss. She was far shorter than her lover, but Kace had fought with her in the arena, and she was a hell of a fighter. Watching the two of them together made something in Kace's chest tighten.

Love was a foreign concept on Antar. In fact, it was expressly forbidden. It was fascinating to see the emotion shining off this couple.

Another woman moved forward. Dr. Regan Forrest was even shorter than Harper. Her flowing white dress accented her full curves and billowed out as she threw herself into Thorin's brawny arms.

Kace resisted shaking his head. Of all the gladiators in the House of Galen, he would never have picked big, wild Thorin to fall for a tiny, sweet Earth girl.

Unwillingly, Kace's gaze searched for the final woman from Earth.

There she was. Aurora Fraser, better known as Rory.

She was short as well, but somewhere between Regan and Harper in height. She didn't have Regan's curves, or Harper's athletic physique. She was built straight up and down, with slim hips, and toned arms. She wasn't wearing a dress like Regan, or fighting leathers like Harper. Instead, she wore simple black trousers and a white shirt that wrapped around her body, hugging small, high breasts. Her unique red hair fell in a wild tangle of curls around her face. Green-gold eyes watched everyone and everything, and a faint smile flirted on her lips.

She'd suffered horribly at the hands of the Thraxians. Then, they'd sold her to the deplorable Vorn. She'd been beaten, treated worse than an animal, but here she was, smiling.

The women of Earth were tough, stubborn, and strong.

Her green-gold gaze met his and she moved closer. "Ready to fight, pretty boy?"

"Always." He fought the urge to tell her not to use that silly name. He was an Antarian soldier, there was nothing pretty about him. She'd called him that from the moment he'd rescued her in the House of Vorn. She'd also given him a black eye during the rescue.

If there was one thing Kace had already learned about Rory Fraser, it was that she swung her fists first and asked questions later.

She boldly eyed him up and down. "I believe it. I'm excited to see you fight."

Kace paused for a second, absorbing the fact that she was going to be watching him tonight. Something inside him liked that.

"Do you get nervous?" she asked.

"No."

He saw her nose wrinkle, and that drew his attention to the interesting splash of dots across the bridge of it. Freckles, she called them.

"Not at all?"

"No." Antarian soldiers didn't feel nerves.

She rolled her eyes. "Okay, gladiator. Well, be careful out there."

"All right, time to move," Galen called out.

Kace gave Rory a nod, even as he noted Raiden planting a huge kiss on Harper. Kace wondered for a brief second what Rory's lips felt like.

Then he shook his head and turned. Sex wasn't outlawed on Antar, nor was it endorsed. Soldiers were encouraged to pour all their emotions into their training, not frivolous activities.

He walked out of the tunnel, lifting his staff and centering his thoughts.

Together, the House of Galen gladiators stepped out onto the sand.

Around them, rows and rows of arena seats were packed full of people. When the crowd saw them, they roared their approval.

Thorin shook his axe in the air, while Saff pumped her fists at the crowd. Lore did a turn and tossed something in the air. Fireworks flew upward and broke off in all directions in silver and red—the House of Galen colors. Nero scowled at him.

Raiden barely paid the crowd any attention, his red cloak flaring behind him as he strode into the heart of the arena. He'd never pandered to the spectators, and he'd still become champion. He was a warrior at heart, and Kace followed his example.

As the others called out to the crowd, Kace knelt and picked up a handful of sand. He let it run through his fingers. He never let himself forget that here, he would be tested and challenged. These weren't fights to the death, but injuries always happened. Blood would splatter the sand. He wasn't here for the glory, he was here for duty and honor.

The tenor of the crowd changed, and Kace straightened.

Their opponents had entered the arena.

He moved to join his team, and saw the Thraxian gladiators coming toward them. Not all the warriors in the House of Thrax were Thraxians, but tonight, most of them were.

They made an impact. Seven feet tall, with powerful muscled bodies, the Thraxians had tough, brown skin, and a set of black horns on their heads. Their eyes glowed orange, and it matched the glow of orange veins visible through their skin.

Saff stepped up beside him. "Ready, military man?"

"Ready."

As the Thraxian gladiators moved into a jog, loping toward them, Raiden turned, a hard look on his face. "For honor and freedom."

"For honor and freedom." Kace raised his voice to join the others. They broke into a run and raced to meet the enemy.

Kace swung his staff, cracking it against the sword of a Thraxian fighter. He spun, bending one knee, and moving his staff upward. It was a fast move, and the Thraxian barely had time to react. The weapon slammed into the alien's side. With a roar, he staggered backward.

Again, Kace swung his staff, and again. His weapon was like an extension of himself. Soon, the Thraxian fell to his knees in the sand, and Kace brought the staff down on the back of the man's neck.

Thwack. The Thraxian plummeted to the sand. Kace leaped over the top of the fallen man and kept moving. He flanked Saff, and they both stared up at the giant Thraxian charging at them. He towered over both of them.

The female gladiator lifted a small, egg-shaped device. Kace nodded and watched as she tossed it at the giant.

The device exploded outward, and a wire-mesh net flew at their opponent. It tangled around his lower half, tripping him over. As he struggled, Kace leaped up, his staff raised above his head. He swung it down and slammed it against the man's lower back. He heard the crack of bones, and the Thraxian roared.

"Nice work." Saff slapped Kace's arm.

They continued to fight through the crowd of gladiators. Nero and Lore fought with determination and a lethal grace. Thorin and Raiden plowed through their opponents.

Finally, Kace pulled to a stop, as Thorin and Raiden engaged the last of the Thraxians. Kace rested the end of his staff in the sand and looked toward the stands.

His gaze zeroed in on the House of Galen seats, down close to the arena floor. Instantly, he spotted that brilliant glow of red hair. He saw that Rory was watching him, grinning.

"Incoming," Saff called out.

Kace whipped his head back and saw a gladiator had broken free from Thorin and Raiden. He was racing toward Saff and Kace. This one was a Gavia. A reptilian species that could spit poison.

Saff tossed her net device up and down in her palm, watching and waiting. When she got like this, she reminded Kace of a hunting cat, patient and cunning.

Usually, Saff was all fire and unrelenting power when she fought. Patience was Kace's skill, not Saff's. More often than not, she charged in without planning.

But this time, Kace didn't want to wait. He felt an extra rush of energy this evening, a need to show off his skills. He rushed forward to meet the gladiator.

Kace used his most dramatic moves, swinging his staff in a wild, lethal dance. He wore the other man down, slamming the staff into him at all the sensitive spots on the Gavia's body. The alien groaned, swinging wildly and spitting green blood onto the sand. His movements were slowing, losing coordination.

Then Kace swung the staff sideways, taking the Gavia down at the knees. He swung again and caught the alien under his jaw, slamming his head back. As the Gavia cursed, he moved his head, and a shower of dark-green poison sprayed out of the alien's mouth.

Kace dived, rolled through the sand, and came back up on his feet. He could hear the poison sizzling on the sand. Again, he swung his staff around and caught the Gavia in the back. The alien fell forward on his hands and knees, struggling to get back up. Then, finally, he collapsed.

The crowd went wild.

Saff appeared beside him, one dark brow arched. "Well, look who ate his Wheaties today."

Kace frowned. *Wheaties?* "I don't know what you're talking about."

"It's a phrase that Regan taught me. Means you ate something that gave you some extra energy today."

Kace didn't respond. Another House of Thrax gladiator was back up, and lumbering toward them. He was big, muscles bulging across his broad chest and wide shoulders. His name was Naare, a Varinid from the planet Varin. He'd been a gladiator with the House of Thrax for years. Kace kind of liked the guy, and knew he had almost earned his freedom. He was very good with an axe.

Naare engaged, swinging his weapon in a wild arc. Saff and Kace ducked and rolled.

Kace spun, bringing his staff up. He struck Naare in the side, then the shoulder.

Kace frowned. The Varinid was usually lightning-fast on his feet. Today, he was slower than a green recruit. Again and again, Kace swung his staff into his opponent, while the other man never got a hit near him.

Naare's eyes were dull. Another two hits of the

staff, and the gladiator went down.

Kace frowned. Naare was close to gaining his freedom, and he usually was a challenging opponent.

But tonight, something was different. Maybe Naare had picked up a drug habit? Kor Magna drew spectators from around the galaxy for the fights, but outside the arena walls, the city—and its shiny, glitzy District—catered to a lot of vices. Gambling, drugs, women, men…whatever you wanted, you could find it here. Kace was well aware more than one gladiator in the arena dealt with their demons through the use of chemicals.

Suddenly, the wail of a siren echoed out over the arena. He heard the announcers calling out, declaring the House of Galen the winners.

Kace wiped his arm across his face, brushing away the blood and sweat. Right here, right now in this moment, he felt a clarity he rarely felt anywhere else.

On Antar, with his squad of soldiers, he'd always felt part of a team, fighting to protect their planet.

But it wasn't until he'd come to the arena that he'd truly felt alive. Here in the arena, he'd learned a lot—about fighting, about strategy, about people. What he hadn't expected was to make friends.

A big fist punched into his shoulder. "Hey there, military man." Thorin hit him again. "What got into you tonight?"

Raiden slid his sword back into his scabbard. "You used some pretty fancy moves out there."

Kace shrugged. "I was in the mood."

"You were just showing off," Saff teased.

"An Antarian soldier does not show off."

His friends continued to rib him as they crossed the sand. As they neared the tunnel, he looked up at the House of Galen seats. He saw Rory at the railing watching him. She was jumping up and down, her arms above her head. He watched as she put her fingers to her mouth and let out a shrill whistle.

Kace's gut hardened as realization set in. *Drak.* It hadn't just been a need to test his skills. The reason he'd acted out of character was sitting in the stands, celebrating his win.

Galactic Gladiators
Gladiator
Warrior
Hero
Protector

Also by Anna Hackett

Treasure Hunter Security
Undiscovered
Uncharted
Unexplored
Unfathomed

Galactic Gladiators
Gladiator
Warrior
Hero
Protector

Hell Squad
Marcus
Cruz
Gabe
Reed
Roth
Noah
Shaw
Holmes
Niko
Finn
Devlin

The Anomaly Series
Time Thief
Mind Raider
Soul Stealer
Salvation
Anomaly Series Box Set

The Phoenix Adventures
Among Galactic Ruins
At Star's End
In the Devil's Nebula
On a Rogue Planet
Beneath a Trojan Moon
Beyond Galaxy's Edge
On a Cyborg Planet
Return to Dark Earth
On a Barbarian World
Lost in Barbarian Space
Through Uncharted Space

Perma Series
Winter Fusion

The WindKeepers Series
Wind Kissed, Fire Bound
Taken by the South Wind
Tempting the West Wind
Defying the North Wind
Claiming the East Wind

Standalone Titles
Savage Dragon
Hunter's Surrender
One Night with the Wolf

Anthologies
A Galactic Holiday
Moonlight (UK only)
Vampire Hunter (UK only)
Awakening the Dragon (UK Only)

For more information visit AnnaHackettBooks.com

About the Author

I'm a USA Today bestselling author and I'm passionate about *action romance*. I love stories that combine the thrill of falling in love with the excitement of action, danger and adventure. I'm a sucker for that moment when the team is walking in slow motion, shoulder-to-shoulder heading off into battle.

I write about people overcoming unbeatable odds and achieving seemingly impossible goals. I like to believe it's possible for all of us to do the same.

My books are mixture of action, adventure and sexy romance and they're recommended for anyone who enjoys fast-paced stories where the boy wins the girl at the end (or sometimes the girl wins the boy!)

For release dates, action romance info, free books, and other fun stuff, sign up for the latest news here:

Website: AnnaHackettBooks.com

Made in the USA
Las Vegas, NV
24 February 2021

18516321R00132